THIRD TIME'S THE CHARM

Locked together, they strained with all their strength, Strath to use his knives, Fargo to prevent him.

Fargo bucked in an effort to heave Strath off but the killer clung on. Hissing, Strath threw all his weight into forcing the tips of his knives into Fargo's neck.

Water lapped at Fargo's ears. He drove his knee into Strath, once, twice, three times. At the third blow Strath let out a howl, wrenched loose, and jumped up and back.

Fargo kicked him in the groin. . . .

THE TRAILSMAN

#331

NORTHWOODS NIGHTMARE

by
Jon Sharpe

A SIGNET BOOK

SIGNET
Published by New American Library, a division of
Penguin Group (USA) Inc., 375 Hudson Street,
New York, New York 10014, USA
Penguin Group (Canada), 90 Eglinton Avenue East, Suite 700, Toronto,
Ontario M4P 2Y3, Canada (a division of Pearson Penguin Canada Inc.)
Penguin Books Ltd., 80 Strand, London WC2R 0RL, England
Penguin Ireland, 25 St. Stephen's Green, Dublin 2,
Ireland (a division of Penguin Books Ltd.)
Penguin Group (Australia), 250 Camberwell Road, Camberwell, Victoria 3124,
Australia (a division of Pearson Australia Group Pty. Ltd.)
Penguin Books India Pvt. Ltd., 11 Community Centre, Panchsheel Park,
New Delhi - 110 017, India
Penguin Group (NZ), 67 Apollo Drive, Rosedale, North Shore 0632,
New Zealand (a division of Pearson New Zealand Ltd.)
Penguin Books (South Africa) (Pty.) Ltd., 24 Sturdee Avenue,
Rosebank, Johannesburg 2196, South Africa

Penguin Books Ltd., Registered Offices:
80 Strand, London WC2R 0RL, England

First published by Signet, an imprint of New American Library,
a division of Penguin Group (USA) Inc.

First Printing, May 2009
10 9 8 7 6 5 4 3 2 1

The first chapter of this book previously appeared in *Tucson Temptress*, the three hundred
thirtieth volume in this series.

Copyright © Penguin Group (USA) Inc., 2009
All rights reserved

 REGISTERED TRADEMARK—MARCA REGISTRADA

Printed in the United States of America

The Trailsman

Beginnings ... they bend the tree and they mark the man. Skye Fargo was born when he was eighteen. Terror was his midwife, vengeance his first cry. Killing spawned Skye Fargo, ruthless, cold-blooded murder. Out of the acrid smoke of gunpowder still hanging in the air, he rose, cried out a promise never forgotten.

The Trailsman they began to call him all across the West: searcher, scout, hunter, the man who could see where others only looked, his skills for hire but not his soul, the man who lived each day to the fullest, yet trailed each tomorrow. Skye Fargo, the Trailsman, the seeker who could take the wildness of a land and the wanting of a woman and make them his own.

The spectacular wilds of British Columbia, 1861—
where the trails were few but the ways to die were many.

1

Skye Fargo saw the black bear before it saw him.

A big man, broad of shoulder and narrow at the hips, he sat tall in the saddle. He spotted the bear when it came out of the thick woods onto the trail and stopped.

Fargo quickly drew rein. He wasn't too concerned. He had a Colt strapped around his waist, over his buckskins. In a sheath in his boot nestled a razor-edged Arkansas toothpick. The splash of white and black under him was an Ovaro. Fargo had been riding the stallion for years now and would go on riding it until it died or he did. He'd never had a horse so dependable.

Fargo waited for the bear to move on. That it was a black bear and not a griz was in his favor. Black bears rarely attacked people. This one was big, though, as big as any he ever came across. But then, the bears were like everything else in the colony of British Columbia.

Fargo didn't know what it was—the land, the water, the soil, the fact there were so few people—but the wildlife and the plant life all seemed to be bigger north of the border.

An old-timer once told Fargo that was the way it had been in the States back in the old days. Where humans were few, the animals grew and grew. Then waves of emigrants, pushing west, killed off the big ones, and the game that came along after that never got the chance to grow as big as those before. They were killed off to fill supper pots and so their pelts could be made into clothes and rugs.

Fargo liked that part about few humans. He was fond of the quiet places, the lonely places, the places hardly any whites ever saw. It was why folks called him the Trailsman. It was why the army relied on him so often as a scout. It was why others hired him as a guide.

That was what Fargo was doing at the moment: guiding. A quarter of a mile back down the trail came his party. He'd gone on ahead to check the trail and keep an eye out for game, and now this black bear had come along and brought him to a stop.

It was late afternoon and Fargo had spent all day in the saddle. He could use a cup of coffee and a hot meal. Stretching, he idly gazed at pillowy clouds floating through the blue British Columbia sky. Then he glanced up the trail and gave a start.

The black bear was coming toward him.

Fargo dropped his hand to his Colt. He'd rather avoid the bear than shoot it. Bears took a lot more butchering than deer, and some people weren't as fond of bear meat as they were of venison. Personally, he liked bear meat just fine, but some of those in the party he was guiding struck him as finicky.

The bear was still coming.

Fargo rose in the stirrups and hollered, "Skedaddle, you idiot." Black bears were skittish. They often ran at the sound of a human voice. But not this one. It raised its nose and sniffed a few times and then kept on lumbering toward him.

"Hell." Fargo reined around and tapped his spurs. He would go back down the trail. The bear would realize he wasn't a threat and go its merry way. He went around a bend and glanced back.

The bear came trotting after him.

"Son of a bitch." Fargo scowled. The bear was moving fast—not a full-out lope, but fast. Clearly, it had decided that he or the Ovaro was worth catching. And what a bear could catch, it ate.

2

Fargo used his spurs again, bringing the stallion to a trot. He trotted around the next bend and went fifty more yards besides, and again drew rein. Surely, he told himself, the black bear had given up.

Here it came, lumbering after him.

"Damn contrary critter." Fargo was mad. He was trying his best to spare the thing and it wanted him for its dinner. Once more he wheeled and this time he rode a good distance at a full gallop, enough to show the bear it had no chance of catching him. Bears were as fast as horses over short spurts, but a horse with a big enough lead usually left a bear eating its dust.

Fargo came to a stop and reined broadside to the trail. He figured that was the end of it. He figured the bear had given up and gone off into the forest in search of easier prey. He waited to be proven right—and was proven wrong.

Once more the black bear appeared, and when it saw him, it ran faster.

Enough was enough. The day Fargo couldn't outsmart a bear was the day he hung up his Colt, found himself a rocking chair somewhere, and put himself out to pasture. He galloped to the next turn and on around. Once out of the bear's sight, he reined into the trees. The undergrowth was so thick, it only took him a few moments to find cover where he could see the trail without being seen.

The seconds went by and Fargo began to think that this time the bear had gotten it through its thick head that it couldn't catch him, when there it was, its heavy paws thudding on the ground. Breathing like a bellows, it ran past his hiding place and soon was out of sight around the next bend.

Chuckling, Fargo gigged the Ovaro and turned up the trail to continue on his way. With the bear behind him he had nothing to worry about. But then it hit him. The bear was now between him and those he was guiding—*and heading right toward them.*

Fargo wheeled the Ovaro. The odds of the bear attacking a

party as large as his was small, but this bear wasn't acting as a bear should. He spurred to a trot, confident he would soon catch up.

Minutes went by, and there was no sign of the bear. Fargo grew more and more sure the bear had given up and gone off into the forest. He was congratulating himself on outsmarting it when the first shot cracked, and then another. There was a roar, and someone screamed.

The bear was attacking them.

Blistering the air with fiery oaths, Fargo sped to their aid. From the shrieks and the cries, at least one person was down and there might be more. Most were city dwellers and prone to panic at a time like this, and too often panic led to dead.

Fargo reached down and shucked his Henry rifle from the saddle scabbard. The brass receiver gleamed as he levered a round into the chamber. The bear was as good as dead. It just didn't know it yet.

Another scream knifed the air. The bear must be wreaking havoc. Then a rifle boomed like a cannon.

McKern's Sharps, Fargo reckoned, and he smiled. A heavy-caliber Sharps could drop most anything in its tracks. No doubt the bear was dead.

A roar proved him wrong.

That might mean McKern was down, too. Fargo hoped not. The old man was the one of two people in that bunch he counted on.

Fargo swept around a bend and then around another and came on a scene straight from every guide's worst nightmare.

The bear must have torn into them before they realized it was there. Three horses were down, whinnying and thrashing and kicking, one with blood spurting from a clawed throat. Their riders were down, too, and two weren't moving. The third was McKern. The old man was pinned under his animal and struggling to pull his leg free.

Fury flooded through Fargo. He wished now he had shot

the damn bear the moment he saw it. There it was, in a wild melee of men and horses, tearing into the rest of the party like a wolverine gone berserk. He snapped the Henry's stock to his shoulder, but a plunging horse filled his sights and he jerked the rifle down again.

A woman wailed in terror.

Angeline Havard was desperately trying to rein her mare out of the bear's path but the petrified mare was slow to respond and paid a fearful cost for its fright.

Roaring in bestial bloodlust, the black bear raked the mare from shoulder to belly, its claws shredding hide and flesh and ripping wide. The mare whinnied and frantically sought to escape.

In a bound the bear had its jaws clamped on the mare's neck.

Angeline screamed. She pushed against her saddle to throw herself clear but the mare stumbled and went down. Her yellow hair flying, Angeline pitched hard to the ground. But she was up on her hands and knees in a twinkling.

The black bear saw her. It let go of the mare's throat and started to clamber over the mare to get at Angeline.

Fargo flew past McKern. The old man hollered something about "blowing out that damn varmint's wick." Fargo didn't catch all of it. He raised the Henry and took aim as best he could with the Ovaro moving under him. He fixed a bead on the back of the black bear's head. Not an ideal shot, given how thick bear skulls were, but he must divert its attention from Angeline.

The bear's maw gaped wide and it went to leap on the helpless girl.

Fargo fired, worked the lever, fired again.

With a roar of pain, the bear spun and hurtled toward him.

Fargo hauled on the reins and brought the stallion to a slewing stop. He fired a third and a fourth time.

The bear didn't slow.

Quickly, Fargo took better aim. He had a front-on shot. He

might be able to hit a lung or the heart but the slug had to go through a lot of muscle and fat. He fired at its eyes, instead.

The Henry held fifteen rounds. He had already squeezed off six; now he squeezed off two more.

The bear became an ursine blur of fangs, claws, and hair.

Fargo banged off another shot.

Slowing, the bear shook its head, as a man might at the stings of a bee. Suddenly it reared onto its hind legs and kept coming.

Which suited Fargo just fine; he had the heart and lung shots he wanted. He fired, fired, fired, the Henry kicking with every blast.

Behind him McKern's Sharps thundered.

The Ovaro, superbly trained, stayed perfectly still. Its eyes were wide and its nostrils were flaring but it didn't bolt.

Fargo had lost count of his shots but he knew he only had one or two left. Another moment, and the bear would be on him. Its eyes were dark pits of animal hate.

That was when Rohan ran up. Rohan, filthy as sin, filthy clothes and filthy skin, with the fancy English shotgun he told everyone he won in a poker game. Rohan, the man in charge of the packhorses. He pointed his shotgun at the black bear's head and blew the top of the bear's skull off.

For a few seconds the bear stayed erect. That was how long it took the body to react to the fact it no longer had a brain. The bear keeled over, hitting the ground with a thud, gore oozing from the cavity in its cranium.

Rohan puffed on the wisps of smoke rising from the muzzle of his shotgun, and chortled. "Did you see that? This baby of mine would drop an elephant."

"Seen a lot of elephants, have you?" Fargo had seen one once, with a traveling circus. The thing nearly killed him.

"No. But I ain't ignorant. I know what elephants are."

Fargo had forgotten how prickly the man could be. "Don't get your dander up. You did just fine."

"I'd have been here sooner but some of the packhorses tried to run off, and I figured saving our food and our bullets was more important than saving any of you."

"Don't let the man who hired us hear you say that."

"Hear him say what?" Theodore Havard demanded, striding up with his spare frame rigid and his shoulders thrown back, as was his habit. He had the air of a man who owned the world. In reality, he owned most of San Francisco.

"We were talking about that," Fargo said with a nod at the dead black bear. "Where were you in all the commotion?"

"My horse threw me and ran off. It's fortunate I wasn't trampled or didn't break a bone."

"Two of the men were mauled."

"They are? I didn't notice."

The rest were gathering. There was Edith Havard, Theodore's shrewish wife. There was Allen, twenty-five and unmarried. Shapely Angeline, younger by four years, brushing grass from her dress.

As for the hirelings, besides Fargo and McKern and Rohan, there were eight others. Or six, if the two prone figures and the spreading pools of blood under them were any indication.

McKern came up, reloading his Sharps. "I have half a mind to shoot this damn critter again. It killed my horse, and I had that animal going on six years now."

"That a shame," Rohan said. "A good horse is special. Hell, any horse is better than people."

"Better how?" McKern responded.

"I'd rather sleep with a horse than a person any day."

McKern took a step back. "Has anyone ever told you that you're a mite weird?"

Of all of them, Allen Havard was the least flustered. He sat his expensive saddle, immaculate in a riding outfit that cost more than most men earned in a year, and sniffed in distaste. "Are you two buffoons done?"

"Sorry, Mr. Havard," McKern said.

7

Allen smirked at his father. "I knew it would come to this. I just knew it. I told you, didn't I, before we ever left home."

"Don't start, boy," Theodore said sternly.

"I'm a *man*, Father, and I'll thank you to treat me like one."

"Must we bicker like this in public?" Edith asked.

Rohan drew a hunting knife and hunkered next to the black bear. He pried its mouth open and began to dig at the gums.

"My word!" Edith exclaimed. "What in heaven's name do you think you're doing?"

"This critter doesn't need its teeth anymore. I aim to make them into a right smart necklace."

Allen Havard uttered a sharp bark that passed for a laugh. "You should have listened to me, Father. I just hope to God this isn't an omen. If it is, we're all doomed."

2

Born in New Jersey, Theodore Havard spent every moment he could at the shore. He loved the sea. At fourteen he hired on as a cabin boy and sailed the world, working his way up the nautical chain until he was a captain of his own ship, which happened to dock in San Francisco. He saw that the once-sleepy little Spanish settlement was destined for great things, and as San Francisco grew, so did his shipping concerns. He became the king of San Francisco shipping. Wisely, he invested a large portion of his profits in real estate, doubling and tripling his wealth. Now it could truly be said that Theodore Havard had everything.

It included a wife who was ten years older. Edith had been working as a clerk in a waterfront store when Theodore set eyes on her and decided she was the woman for him. No one could figure out exactly what he saw in her. She was plain, for one thing, and constantly carped, for another. To be fair, she carped about everything, and not just him.

They had three children.

Allen, the dandy, loved fine clothes and fine food and fine entertainment. He saw himself as urbane and the rest of humanity as clods. That his father made him work for his money annoyed him considerably. Allen regarded work as beneath him.

Angeline was the youngest. If her parents weren't surprised that they gave birth to such a beauty, everyone else was. Angeline was stunning. Her golden hair shimmered as if it were the sun. Her complexion was flawless, her eyes a bright emerald green. Then there was her hourglass body. Fargo had admired that body often. He admired it nearly every time he glanced at her on the long journey north.

Kenneth Havard was the oldest, and the one Fargo had yet to meet. Kenneth was, by all accounts, sober and hardworking. As his father before him had gone off to see the world and make something of himself, Kenneth decided to do the same. But where his father loved the sea, Kenneth liked his feet on solid ground. When he heard of the Fraser Canyon gold rush in the British colony of British Columbia, he did as thousands of Americans had done, and hastened north to make his fortune.

Amazingly, Kenneth found gold. Most did not. Most dug and panned hour after hour and day after day and ended up with nothing but calluses and disappointment.

Kenneth survived the so-called Fraser Canyon War, and when many of the disappointed greedy later left, he stayed on to work his claim. A dutiful son, he wrote regular letters home. His mother begged him to pay them a visit but he pleaded he couldn't take the time.

Four months ago the letters had stopped.

Theodore Havard sent an inquiry to the British authorities to find out why. The reply—that their son had gone missing—shocked Theordore and Edith so much, they decided to travel to British Columbia and investigate. They needed a guide. British Columbia was sparsely populated, Fraser Canyon remote. To get there they had to pass through untamed and largely unexplored country. They needed someone who knew the wilds and wildlife and wild men, white and red, who would as soon slit a traveler's throat as talk to him.

As fate would have it, Fargo happened to be in San Francisco playing poker, wetting his throat with whiskey, and being as friendly as he could be to doves who caught his eye. Luck, ever a fickle mistress, drained his poke. So when

Havard's man Cosmo sought him out and offered him the job and after some dickering offered to pay him three times what he would normally make as a guide, Fargo accepted.

Fargo didn't know what to make of Cosmo. Edith referred to him as their butler but Cosmo was much more. He dressed Theodore. He shaved Theodore. He fed Theodore. He ran errands and handled business matters. He was more like a wife than a butler, and more like a wife than Edith. Perhaps that explained why they couldn't stand each other.

The expedition, as Allen liked to call it, numbered seventeen, counting Fargo and the Havards and Cosmo, but now, thanks to the black bear that thought it was a grizzly, they were down to fifteen.

McKern had been everywhere and done everything. He was a good shot with that Sharps of his. He was fond of liquor and cards. Of all of them, Fargo liked McKern the most.

Rohan loved horses. They were all he cared about. He never went anywhere without his shotgun. And he never, ever took a bath.

Of the others, there was one Fargo didn't like. His name was Strath. He had a ferret face and ferret eyes and wore two knives, one on either hip. He wore a cap and seaman's garb and supposedly had worked as a crewman on several ships. He knew nothing about British Columbia and less about the wilds, and why Cosmo hired him, Fargo couldn't say. But something about the man made the skin on his back prickle whenever Strath was standing behind him.

So here they were, well on their way, and well north of the border. After Cosmo spoke a few words over the two dirt mounds about souls and eternity, they resumed their long trek.

Fargo was in the lead, the rest trailing after him in single file. They had only gone a short way when hooves thudded and Angeline came up next to him, her golden tresses cascading over her shoulders, a warm smile on her luscious lips.

"That was awful brave of you back there."

"What was?" Fargo couldn't think of anything particularly courageous he had done. He was only doing what he was hired to do.

"That way you charged that bear. My heart was in my throat."

"I didn't know you cared."

Angeline blushed and looked away and then looked back again. "It's just that we can't afford to have anything happen to you. Cosmo says you are—what was the word he used? Oh, yes. Indispensable."

"Cosmo said that?"

"I heard him with my own ears. He has heard a lot about you from somewhere. He says you are one of the best scouts alive, and that Father was fortunate to hire you."

"Well, now."

"Frankly, I'm glad you're along. You're one of the few I can talk to. Mr. Rohan stinks to high heaven. Mr. Strath is always undressing me with his eyes. The rest are too nervous around a woman. Except for Mr. McKern. He's a dear. Did you know he has six children and fourteen grandchildren? His wife passed on last year, the poor man."

Fargo let her prattle. Strath wasn't the only one who liked to undress her with his eyes, and she had a nice voice, besides.

"Can I ask you something?" Angeline said.

"I've lost count."

"What?"

"You were about to ask me how many women I've slept with," Fargo said with a grin. "I've lost count."

Angeline blushed again, but laughed. "You sure do enjoy teasing me. But no, that isn't what I wanted to ask." She sobered. "Do you think my brother Kenneth is still alive?"

"I can't predict." As Fargo understood it, the word Theodore got back from the British was that his son had gone off somewhere and never come back.

"Allen doesn't. Allen thinks we're wasting our time and

our money. Especially our money. But that's Allen for you. He never thinks of anyone except himself."

"I'm surprised he came along."

"Oh, he didn't want to. You should have heard him squawk when Father and Mother told him he was coming and that was that. He's too fond of his fine restaurants and the theater and the gay life he likes to live. Now here he is in the middle of nowhere." Angeline chuckled. "And on a horse, no less. Allen hates to ride. He says it chafes him."

"Maybe he should tie a pillow to his saddle."

Angeline laughed. "Don't give him ideas. He had a custom seat made for his carriage so it's softer than most." She sighed. "Sometimes I think he was born in the wrong body."

"And your other brother?" Fargo was curious.

"Kenneth is the opposite. He likes to ride, to hunt, to fish. Growing up, he would rather be outdoors than indoors. I wasn't at all surprised when he announced he was joining the gold rush. The adventure and the hardship would appeal to him."

"So he can take care of himself?"

"Can he ever! Kenneth could live off the land if he had to. When we were little, Cosmo took us camping a few times. Allen hated it but Kenneth loved it. He told me that when he grew up, he would like nothing better than to live by himself off in the mountains somewhere."

"A gent after my own heart."

"You'll like him, yes." Worry came over her. "Provided he's still alive. It's been months. Surely we would have heard something by now."

More hooves drummed and Allen Havard paced the Ovaro on the other side. "What are you two talking about?"

"None of your business," Angeline told him.

"My, my, aren't we prickly today? But not asking for myself. Mother sent me. I gather she doesn't care to have you associate with our frontiersman."

"I'm a grown woman. I can do as I want."

Allen held up a hand. "You'll get no argument from me, dear sister. She doesn't approve of much that I do, either." He focused on Fargo. "Father tells me you can track as good as an Indian."

"Better than most." Fargo wasn't bragging, just stating fact. "I've had a lot of experience."

"Better you than me." Allen gazed out over the pristine valley and the virgin forest that mantled the higher slopes, and frowned. "Look at all this waste. I fail to see the appeal."

"It's beautiful here," Angeline disagreed.

"If you're a chipmunk or an owl. Give me the Imperial Theater and a production of *As You Like It* any day."

Fargo looked at him. "You hate the wilds that much?"

"What good is it? Trees, trees, and more trees. Animals and birds all over the place. Fish dirtying the water. Bugs that sting and bite. What purpose does any of it serve?"

"That's a ridiculous question," Angeline said. "The natural world just *is*. As for its purpose, trees are cut down for wood to build homes. The animals fill our bellies and clothe us. And even you fished once or twice when you were a boy."

"You forgot the bugs," Allen said, and smirked. "But my point, dear sister, is that in the greater scheme of things, the natural world, as you call it, can't compare to the world we make. Contrast a backwoods bumpkin like Rohan to a cultured gentleman and it should be obvious."

"And by cultured you mean you?"

Allen indulged in a smug grin. "If the shoe fits." He gestured at Fargo. "I leave it to you, sir. Name one advantage these pathetic wilds have over civilization."

"You run into a lot fewer jackasses who are full of themselves."

Angeline snorted.

Allen glared, then wheeled his horse and rode back along the line to his mother.

"I'm afraid my brother will hold that against you forever. He never, ever forgets an insult."

"He knows where to find me."

"Oh, no, he would never dare to confront you. Not face-to-face. He's never been in a fight in his life. But he's paid others to fight for him. And maybe worse." Angeline's lovely features clouded. "Once, about five years ago, it was, he got into a terrible row at an establishment called the Gilded Palace. A gambler accused him of cheating and slapped him around. Everyone was talking about it. About a month later the gambler's body washed up onshore. Someone beat him to death and threw him in the sea and the tide carried his body back in again."

"You think your brother was to blame?"

"I wouldn't put anything past Allen. He might seem puny but never underestimate him."

Just what Fargo needed, to have to watch his back as well as watch out for everyone else. When he was hired, he told Theodore Havard that he would do his best to get them all alive to Fraser Canyon.

"What are you thinking about?" Angeline asked.

Fargo decided to test the waters. "How you would look without that dress on."

"Oh my." Angeline blushed the deepest red yet. "No one has ever said a thing like that to me."

"They must not have many men in San Francisco."

"Nonsense. Men are all over. They just don't go around making suggestive remarks to ladies, is all."

"What do they do when they want to make love to a woman? Send her a formal invite?"

"The things you say!" Angeline declared. But she laughed. "Are all frontiersman so bold?"

"I can't speak for the rest," Fargo said, "but when I see something I like, I'm not shy about saying how much I like it."

For a while Angeline rode in silence. Then she cleared her

throat. "Not that I'm the least bit interested, you understand, but all I would be to you is a dalliance. Isn't that right?"

"I wouldn't ask you to marry me after," Fargo admitted.

"Goodness. A girl can't accuse you of misleading her. But honestly. Do you really think there is any chance at all you and I will do *that*?"

"You're a woman. I'm a man. That's all it takes."

"The very idea is preposterous."

Fargo leaned toward her." Before this is done, I'm going to make you gush."

3

The colony of British Columbia

Fargo had heard tell it was the Queen of England who gave the colony its name. The "Columbia" had to do with the Columbia River, which flowed through the southern part of the colony.

Until about a dozen years ago, there was a dispute between the United States and the Crown over exactly where the boundary should be. But the politicians finally worked it out, and now there was British Columbia north of the line and Oregon Territory below it. In size, British Columbia was bigger than all of Oregon Territory and all of California combined.

The terrain was a lot like the northern half of Oregon Territory. In Fargo's estimation, British Columbia was one of the most spectacular regions on the continent. The coast extended up to Alaska, and there were all sorts of bays and coves where craft could put in. Bordering the coast was lush rain forest— whole areas yet to be explored. Then there were the inner mountain ranges, some of the highest peaks anywhere, heavily timbered and cut by deep canyons and lush valleys.

For being so far north, in the summer much of British Columbia was ungodly hot. Over a hundred degrees in the shade in places like Fraser Canyon, where they were bound.

It went without saying that wildlife was plentiful. Deer were everywhere, elk numerous. Moose favored shadowy forest haunts and wetlands, where they could stay cool. Far to the north caribou roamed.

Black bears, as Fargo had just had confirmed, were as thick as ticks on an old hound, grizzlies only slightly less so. Then there were the mountain lions, the wolves, the wolverines. As well as lesser predators, like coyotes and foxes.

Eagles and hawks soared in the skies. So, too, along the coast and inland waterways, did ospreys.

To Fargo, British Columbia was paradise on earth. It had everything: scenery to stun the senses; game to fill the supper pot; vast tracts waiting to be discovered.

The Hudson's Bay Company had opened up the territory. They had set up a network of trading posts, and some had grown into settlements and towns.

British Columbia also had Indians. Some were friendly; some weren't. The tribe that interested Fargo the most at the moment called themselves the Nlaka'pamux. Most whites called them the Knifes, because when they fought, they liked to get in close and use their razor-sharp blades to deadly effect.

The tribe had been friendly until a few years ago. Then, during the Fraser gold rush, some miners had raped a Knife maiden. Enraged warriors swooped down on those they held to blame and killed them in revenge. It was likely the bodies would never have been discovered, and that would have been the end of it. But the Knifes chopped off the heads and threw the heads in the river. The current carried the heads down to the town of Yale, triggering an uproar. Militia companies were hastily organized, made up mostly of Americans in the area illegally, after gold.

The war was short but fierce. Some of the whites wanted to wipe the Knife Indians out. Others just wanted to teach them not to go around chopping off heads. A lot of Indians were killed. No one knew exactly how many. A lot of whites died, too. No one knew how many of them died, either.

Then the British authorities arrived and put an end to the hostilities.

Bad blood still existed, though. A lot of whites would as soon see the Knife Indians dead. A lot of Knife Indians felt the same about whites. Fargo had checked before leading his party north. An army captain he knew warned him that while the British government kept a tight rein on things, now and then whites disappeared.

They weren't the only ones Fargo had to watch out for.

The Fraser gold rush had run its course and many of the Americans who had flocked to Fraser Canyon had gone back home. But those who struck gold, and a lot of others, stayed on. Some of those others were cutthroats, robbers, and killers from south of the border who liked the fact there was less law north of it.

This, then, was the cauldron of danger into which Fargo was bringing the Havards. A lot of people had tried to talk Theodore Havard out of coming, for his own good and the sake of his family, but Theodore was as stubborn as he was rich, and determined to find out what had happened to his older son. Yes, he was hardheaded, and yes, his money had made him arrogant, but he genuinely cared for his children.

Fargo was bringing them in along one of the inland trails rather than up the coast by boat to Vancouver and then across to Fraser Canyon. The British wanted Americans to enter the colony through Vancouver. They also wanted the Americans to leave their weapons south of the border.

Fargo wasn't about to go anywhere—let alone into a hot-bed of bad blood between white and red, with white badmen thrown into the mix—without his Colt, his Henry, and his Arkansas toothpick.

Another couple of days and they would reach Fraser Canyon. Fargo had been there once and remembered it fairly well. The name was misleading. It wasn't just one canyon. It was divided into the Lower and Upper Fraser Canyons, with many smaller canyons and valleys branching off on both sides of the Fraser River. Some of those smaller canyons had names of

19

their own: the Chum Creek Canyon, the Cayoosh Canyon, the Coquihalla Canyon.

Now, coming to the top of a timbered ridge, Fargo halted. The sun would set soon. Just below was a clearing beside a meandering stream. He had found it earlier when he was scouting ahead, and it would make a perfect campsite.

McKern rode up and drew rein. Gazing out over the high peaks, he scratched his grizzled chin. "From here on out we have to be extra-careful."

"I know."

"These pilgrims you're bringing in are lambs for the slaughter and too dumb to realize it."

"I know that, too."

"It must be nice to know everything."

Fargo chuckled. "It must be nice to be a feisty old grump."

"Now, now. Respect your elders, sonny. I was fighting Blackfeet when you were still in diapers."

"Fighting or running from?"

Cackling, McKern said, "Now see. That's why I like you, young hoss. You're wise beyond your years. Sometimes the smartest way to deal with redskins is to show them your backside."

"If it's kill or run and I have no reason to kill, I light a shuck."

McKern nodded in approval. "That's another thing I like about you. You think before you act, whereas most pups your age act before they think." He lowered his voice. "But I didn't come up here to shower you with compliments. I came to warn you."

Fargo arched an eyebrow.

"What did you do to get Allen Havard so mad? The looks he gives you when your back is turned are downright mean."

"I wasn't as polite as he thought I should be. And looks never hurt anyone."

"If the looks were all there was, I wouldn't be talking to

you." McKern glanced over his shoulder and lowered his voice. "He's been rubbing shoulders with Strath about you."

"How do you know it's about me? Did you hear them?"

"No. When they rubbed shoulders they both gave you looks. They probably figured no one else noticed but I don't miss much."

"Calling a man a jackass isn't cause for him to have you killed."

"Is that what you did? Damn. Wish I had been there. That Allen is about the most weak sister I ever came across. Have you ever shook his hand? It's like shaking hands with the air. There's nothing there. I've had babies with stronger grips."

Fargo laughed.

"He's rich and pampered and soft. He looks down his nose at everyone and everything. And to top it off, he smells like a whorehouse on Saturday night."

"I know."

"Oh. That's right. I keep forgetting. You know everything." McKern lifted his reins. "Well, just wanted you to know you're being thought of. Keep your eyes skinned, hoss."

The ridge at their backs sheltered them from the night wind, which at times was chill and brisk, even in summer. The timber hid their campfires from unfriendly eyes, or so Fargo hoped. The water was cold and clear as only British Columbian water could be.

Cosmo was in charge of setting up their camps. He had men erecting tents, men chopping wood, a man fetching water.

Rohan took care of the horses. That was all he ever did. He tethered and tended them at night; he led the pack string by day. He remarked once to Fargo that he had gotten his start as a horse wrangler down in Texas. Rohan liked horses so much that at night he never slept near a fire like everyone else. He spread out his blankets next to the horse string.

Now Fargo led the Ovaro over. He shucked the Henry from the scabbard and untied his bedroll. Setting them down, he went to loose the cinch so he could strip the saddle and saddle blanket.

"I'll do that," Rohan offered.

"It's my horse."

"I don't mind. You've got a fine animal. As grand a horse as I've seen anywhere." Rohan's admiration was genuine. "I'd give anything to have a horse like yours."

"The roan you ride is no swayback."

Rohan glanced at his own animal. "Julius is the best horse I've ever ridden. I'm as attached to him as you are to yours."

"You gave it a name?"

"Sure. I was on a stage once with a schoolteacher. He loved to hear himself talk. And what he most liked to talk about were a bunch of folks he called the Romans. Maybe you've heard of them? One was a gent by the name of Julius something or other. Anyway, I liked the name so much, I gave it to the roan."

Fargo had never named the Ovaro, nor given names to the horses he owned before it. He supposed he could remedy that but he had gone so long without, what difference did it make?

Three campfires were crackling At one, Cosmo was setting up a bipod and a large black pot. In addition to his duties as butler and as Theodore Havard's manservant, Cosmo also cooked all of Theodore's meals. Not Edith, the wife, or even Angeline, the daughter, but Cosmo.

Fargo went over. "How are you holding up?"

"Never better. I had a few rough moments earlier when that bear attacked. But other than that, I am surprisingly serene." Cosmo looked up from the carrots he was chopping. "I have it from a reliable source that Mrs. Havard and her son are upset with you."

"You, too?" Fargo said.

"Theodore has not heard about it yet. Nor will he, if I have anything to say about it. He has enough to worry about without these petty antics."

Fargo grunted. It was interesting how Cosmo always called Edith "Mrs. Havard" but he always called Theodore "Theodore" and never "Mr. Havard."

"You seem to have upset Angeline, too. She was talking to you awhile, and when she came back and rode past me, I couldn't help but notice she looked as if someone had slapped her."

"That's between her and me."

Cosmo stopped chopping and wagged the big butcher knife. He always wore a black jacket and white shirt, his black hair was always neatly combed, and his shoes somehow always kept polished. "Perhaps I have been remiss."

"Been what?"

"I've neglected to make clear how fond I am of my employer. And his family, too, of course." Cosmo leaned an elbow on his knees and pointed the knife at Fargo. "I have been employed by Theodore for going on twelve years. I take my responsibilities seriously."

"Good for you."

Cosmo acted as if he hadn't heard. "One of those responsibilities is to ensure that Theodore makes it through each day with few impositions on his good nature. Do you follow me?"

"You don't like him upset."

"No, I don't. I don't like it at all. And when the other members of his family are upset, it upsets him. You can see where this is leading."

"I can't help it if Allen is a lunkhead."

"And what about Angeline? Is she a lunkhead, too?" Cosmo resumed his chopping. "Look. I'm not all that fond of Allen, myself. But he is Theodore's son. And Mrs. Havard can be a terrible bore, but she is Theodore's wife. So I would rather that they weren't upset. Because Theodore might become upset, and that would upset me." Cosmo looked up. "And you don't want me upset."

"I'll be damned. Did you just threaten me?"

"Call it whatever you will. The important thing is that you don't cause Theodore trouble. I can't stress how important that is. Because if you do, you won't like the consequences."

Fargo placed his hand on his Colt. "Anytime."

Cosmo blinked, and grinned. "Oh, not here and now. What sort of simpleton do you take me for? Theodore would see us, and that would upset him." He shook his head. "If it comes to that, you and I will go off into the trees and settle our differences in private."

"Anytime," Fargo said again.

"Let's not be tedious. I have been open and honest with you, have I not? Which is more than Allen will be." Cosmo stopped chopping again. "I have nothing against you personally, Mr. Fargo. Theodore says we need you, and that's enough for me. But you would do well to keep in mind that Allen can be headstrong and rash at times."

"One minute you're threatening me and the next you're warning me."

"Consider both warnings, if you want. But watch your back, Mr. Fargo. Watch it very closely, indeed."

4

Fargo always took a turn keeping watch. There were enough men that he had to do it only for two hours every other night. Back in San Francisco, Theodore Havard had mentioned that as their guide, Fargo should be exempt from camp duties. Fargo had responded with thanks but no, thanks—he would do his share, just like everyone else.

"Why not make use of the extra rest?" Theodore had gestured at the men bustling to get the pack animals ready. "Why do you think I pay these people, anyway? This isn't a democracy. They are to do as I say. And if I say you don't have to stand guard, then by God, that's the way it will be."

Fargo had declined a second time.

"I don't understand you. I truly don't. You seem to have forgotten the cardinal rule in life."

"And what would that be?"

"Always look out for yourself before everyone else. Except for family. They're the only exceptions."

Fargo still refused.

"Very well. But I must say, you disappoint me. I am being generous and you throw it in my face."

Now, at two in the morning, a man named Becker woke Fargo to let him know it was his turn. Fargo nodded and slowly sat up, sleep clinging like cobwebs. He shook his head to clear it, then stretched. Casting off his blankets, he stifled a yawn.

The camp was quiet, as it should be. Everyone else was asleep. A few tossed and turned. Snores filled the air.

Fargo went to the campfire. One was always kept going all night. He had cautioned them against making the fires too big. When someone asked why, he had explained that big fires could be seen for miles, and when a war party spotted one, they knew it must be white men.

Fargo poured a cup of coffee. That was another thing that was never neglected. It was Theodore Havard's favorite brand; he wouldn't drink any other. Cosmo mentioned once that it came from South America and cost three times as much as the coffee sold in general stores. Fargo liked it. It had a rich, almost chocolate taste, and never bothered his stomach no matter how much he drank.

Becker had already turned in, a blanket pulled over his head.

Taking his cup and the Henry, Fargo roamed the camp to make sure all was well. He passed the four tents. Theodore and Edith were in one, Angeline in another, and Allen had a third. The fourth, the smallest, was for Cosmo. Fargo never heard of a butler having his own tent, but then, Cosmo was more than a butler. Exactly what Cosmo was, everyone had to figure out on his own.

Fargo did some serious figuring. The key was Edith Havard; she despised Cosmo.

He came to the horses, tethered in a string, most dozing. At the near end slept Rohan, snoring the loudest of anyone. Fargo was tempted to drop bits of grass into Rohan's open mouth, but didn't. Rohan didn't have much of a sense of humor.

A multitude of stars sparkled in the firmament. Wind rustled the pines. From out of the dark came grunts, howls and yips, but at a distance. The smell of the fire, and the people smell, kept the meat eaters away.

Fargo squatted at the fire. He refilled his cup and gratefully sipped. All in all, it hadn't been bad so far. He was being paid a lot more than usual, the food was better than usual, and his employer, and everyone else, left him pretty much alone. He liked it that way.

A soft tread caused Fargo to stiffen and spin, his hand dropping to his Colt. He relaxed when he saw who it was. "What are you doing up?"

"I can't sleep," Angeline replied. She curled her legs under her and eased down. Then she poured a cup of coffee. She didn't look at him until she raised the cup. "It's your fault."

"What did I do?"

"You and your lewd suggestions. I can't get them out of my head."

Fargo grinned. "That's a good sign."

"I don't find this funny. I'm a lady, Mr. Fargo. Maybe that doesn't mean anything to you but it means a great deal to me. I don't go around sleeping with every Tom, Dick, and Harry."

"Who asked you to? There's you and there's me. And we're both grown-ups."

"Should I be flattered?"

"You shouldn't be shocked when a grown man likes you enough to want to please you under the blankets."

A snicker escaped her. "You pick strange words to describe out-and-out lust. It's not me you want to please. It's your own base desires."

"What's base about a man wanting a woman?" Fargo countered in mild annoyance. "Men have been wanting women since there *were* men and women. It's as normal as breathing or eating or sleeping."

"You have it all figured out. I'd never have imagined you were such a philosopher."

"Go to hell."

Angeline drew back as if he had slapped her. "No one has ever talked to me the way you do."

"No, I'd guess most don't. They treat you like a princess. They act like you're special and put you on a pedestal." Fargo took a sip. "If I'm wrong, set me right."

After a moment's hesitation Angeline said, "No. You're not wrong. Everyone is always polite and treats me kindly. I think that's why you fascinate me so."

"I treat you no different than I would any other woman."

"Oh, I'm not saying you've been mean. It's just that you talk to me as a woman and not as a princess, as you put it. You treat me as I am and I'm not used to that."

Fargo remembered what Cosmo told him. "Then I haven't hurt your feelings?"

"I admit you upset me. This is the first time anything like this has happened. Most men are so scared of my father, they walk on eggshells when I'm around. But you're not afraid of anyone or anything, are you?"

"Don't make me out to be more than I am."

"And what are you, exactly?"

"A man."

"That's all? Just a man?"

"I'm a man who would like to kiss every square inch of your body."

Angeline gave another start, then covered her mouth and chortled. "There you go again. Keep this up and I won't get any sleep at all."

Fargo lowered his cup. "Give me half an hour, and you'll be so tired, you can't keep your eyes open."

"You're awful sure of yourself. Tell me. Are you one of those who hungers for every female he meets?"

"Only the ones I like. And I like you a lot."

The next moment a shooting star blazed across the sky. Fargo nodded at the fiery streak and said, "The Sioux consider them an omen. When a man and a woman see one, they're meant to make love."

"You're making that up."

"Damn. You're onto me."

Angeline nearly spilled her coughing laughing. "You're a handful—I'll say that."

"No, you're the handful." Fargo wriggled his fingers. "And I've got the hands."

"For a scout, you are not at all what I expected." Angeline sighed and put her cup down. "I better try to get some sleep. We have another long day in the saddle ahead of us tomorrow."

"We could go for a walk," Fargo suggested, with a nod at the benighted woods.

"Oh, no, you don't. I won't be that easy." Angeline stood. "I admit I'm flattered. And I admit I'm intrigued. This is all so new. A man wanting me." She glanced around, then bent toward him and said quietly, "You might find it hard to believe, but I don't have a lot of experience when it comes to, well, *it*. I've led a sheltered life, Skye. My parents are very protective. My mother especially. So if you really want me, you'll have to be patient with me."

Fargo liked how her breasts swelled against her dress. He liked the hint of willowy thigh. He liked her full red lips. Most of all, he liked the suggestion that if he played his cards right, those lips and breasts and thighs would be his to do with as he wanted. "I'm the most patient gent alive."

"I thought you might be." Grinning, Angeline made for her tent, her hips swinging with each stride.

"Women," Fargo said.

Half an hour went by.

The camp still lay peaceful under the stars.

Fargo rose to make another circuit of the clearing. He passed the tents, the horses. He came to the stream and stood on the bank, listening to the gurgle of the water. Cradling the Henry, he gazed across the valley at the range they must cross tomorrow. It was a steep climb to the next pass.

Fargo wasn't thinking of danger. The night was serene. It gave the illusion that all was well. He couldn't say what made him suddenly glance over his shoulder.

Strath was only a few yards away, stealthily stalking him with a knife in each hand.

With an oath, Fargo whirled and started to level the Henry. But Strath was on him in a bound, one of the knives streaking high, the other low. One glanced off the Henry's barrel. The other missed Fargo's leg by a whisker. He drove the stock at Strath's face but Strath nimbly sprang aside.

Fargo didn't shout for help. This was his fight. Again he went to shoot but Strath sprang in close and cut at his neck and side. Fargo twisted and took a step back—into empty space. He had forgotten he was standing on the bank.

Gravity took over.

It was only a five-foot drop; Fargo hit and rolled. He wound up on his belly, half in and half out of the stream. The Henry was under him. The thump of boots galvanized him into throwing himself to one side. Cold steel flashed past his eyes. He kicked and connected, eliciting a snarl of fury.

But now Fargo was flat on his back and he no longer had the Henry. He clawed for his Colt.

Strath darted in, both knives high, to stab. He slammed his knee down hard on Fargo's chest. Pain exploded. Fargo flung his arms out and seized Strath's wrists as the knives swept toward him. Strath sought to wrest free but Fargo's grip was stonger.

Locked together, they strained with all their strength, Strath to use his knives, Fargo to prevent him.

Fargo bucked in an effort to heave Strath off, but the killer clung on. Hissing, Strath threw all his weight into forcing the tips of his knives into Fargo's neck.

Water lapped at Fargo's ears. He drove his knee into Strath, once, twice, three times. At the third blow Strath let out a howl, wrenched loose, and jumped up and back.

Fargo kicked him in the groin.

"Bastard!" Strath staggered toward the bank but didn't make it. He fell to one knee.

In a blur, Fargo drew his Colt. He swept upright, swinging as he rose, and clubbed Strath across the temple. That was all it took. Grabbing hold of Strath's shirt, Fargo hauled him out of the water.

"Well done."

Fargo glanced up.

Cosmo, wearing a heavy robe, stood at the top of the bank. "Sounds woke me and I came out to see what it was."

"He tried to kill me," Fargo said, breathing heavily.

"I'm glad he failed. It would be difficult to find another guide of your caliber."

"That's all I matter to you?"

"No, that is how you matter to Theodore. To me you don't matter at all." Cosmo put his hands in the robe's pockets. "This is most distressing. It will upset Theodore, and I've already told you how I feel about upsetting him."

"He'll be upset even more when I pistol-whip his son."

"Allen? Whatever for?"

"I suspect he put Strath up to this." Fargo started up the bank. "He has to answer for it."

"Let me help." Cosmo bent and offered his hand.

Not entirely trusting him, Fargo took hold. He had felt some strong grips in his time but few as strong as Cosmo's. The man pulled him up with ridiculous ease.

"There. Now we can talk."

Fargo's buckskins were dripping wet. He took off his hat and shook it. "About what?"

"I prefer that you don't confront Allen just now. We'll bind Strath and turn him over to the British authorities. I'll inform Theodore that Strath was trying to steal from you, and when you caught him, he tried to knife you."

"No."

"What do you have to lose by cooperating? I only want to spare Theodore the pain of having his youngest son charged with attempted murder. Isn't it enough that his oldest son is missing?"

"The answer is still no."

"Don't be so hasty. You see, the sounds that woke me were those of you and Miss Havard having your little discussion. If you agree about Allen, in return, I won't inform Mrs. Havard that you are trying your utmost to seduce her daughter. Were she to find out, she would undoubtedly keep Angeline on a tight leash and not let you anywhere near her."

"You fight dirty."

"I thought you would see things my way."

5

Fargo had two reasons for giving in. The first was that he couldn't prove Allen Havard was behind Strath's attack. He would bide his time, and when he did have the proof, he'd do what he had to. In the meantime Strath had to ride under guard with his ankles bound.

Cosmo told Theodore Havard that Fargo had caught Strath going through the packs with the aim of "pilfering," as Cosmo called it, and when Fargo confronted him, Strath whipped out his knives. At least one person didn't believe the story.

The next morning they had been under way half an hour when McKern brought his mount up alongside the Ovaro.

"That butler sure is slick. If we run out of whale oil for the lanterns, we can fill the lanterns with him."

"Figured it out, have you?"

"See these gray hairs? I didn't get them by being stupid. And remember, I saw Strath talking to Allen."

Above them an eagle soared on outstretched wings. In the woods a jay screeched.

"So are you going to tell me how it really happened?" McKern asked.

"You've never heard of pilfering before?"

"Pilfering, my ass. Where I come from, folks call things what they are. Stealing. Robbing. Even thieving. Only a fancy pants like that butler or whatever he is would call it pilfering."

"Now, now, remember your station."

"Station?" McKern repeated, and roared. "You did that

good. If you had the money to go with a stuck-up nose, you could make something of yourself."

"I like cards and women too much. Any money I make doesn't stick around long."

"You're not alone. I spend money like a cloud spends rain. But, hey, you could always do butlering. There must be good money in that, the way Cosmo dresses. And you'd make a fine one, the words you spout."

"The day I wait on someone hand and foot is the day I'm fit to blow my brains out."

"The trouble with you, sonny, is you ain't been citified."

"I hope to God I never am."

McKern let a minute go by before he said, "So listen. You want me to keep an eye on Allen from here on out? On the sly. There's no telling what he might try next."

"Rabbits don't scare me any, but maybe you better." Fargo wasn't eager for a knife in the back.

"The thing to remember about rabbits is that they'll bite when they're cornered."

"I'm obliged."

"Think nothing of it. Or if you insist, buy me a bottle of red-eye when this is over and we'll call it even."

"Deal." Fargo raised his reins. "I'm going to scout ahead. I should be back by noon. Keep a watch until I get back."

"You can count on me, hoss."

Fargo was glad to get away. He trotted for a while and then slowed to a walk. The trail they were following, one of several used during the gold rush days, was easy to follow.

About ten in the morning Fargo topped a rise. Off to his right was a slope sprinkled with talus. And climbing ponderously up it was the lord of the Rockies: a grizzly.

Fargo was glad the griz was going in the other direction. From the way it was sniffing and nosing about, he reckoned it was after marmots. His hunch was confirmed when the griz came to a dark spot that must be a hole and commenced scooping out great wads of earth with its immense paws. Dirt and rocks flew. A cloud of dust rose.

The bear's massive head half disappeared.

Then came a faint squeal. The grizzly drew its head out and shook it from side to side. Clamped in its iron jaws was the marmot, limp in death.

"Life in a nutshell," Fargo said, and clucked to the Ovaro.

Shortly after Fargo spied some elk in a high meadow. Later still, high on a rocky crag, he saw splashes of brown that might be mountain sheep.

This was Fargo's kind of country. Raw, ripe with life, ruled by the natural law of fang and claw. He could see himself one day, when he was on in years, building a cabin and living out what was left of his life in a place like this. To him it was as close to heaven as anywhere could be.

By now he was half a mile above the valley floor, climbing toward the pass. He wasn't expecting to encounter anyone. So when he went around a bend and spied four men sitting by the side of the trail, it was an unwanted surprise.

Fargo put his hand on his Colt. He liked to think he was a good judge of men, and his judgment told him the four might be trouble. They were scruffy and dirty and had unkempt beards. More important, each man was an armory. Their horses were cropping grass or resting.

Fargo drew rein a good ten feet out.

A block of muscle with an anvil jaw stood. His smile lacked two upper teeth. "Morning, mister," he said amiably enough. "Glorious day, ain't it?"

"Not for marmots," Fargo said.

The man cocked his head. "I don't rightly know what you mean by that, but never you mind. I'm called Bucktooth on account of I don't have any."

Fargo didn't offer his own handle.

"These here are my pards," Bucktooth said with a sweep of his arm. "We're on our way back to the States and stopped to rest a spell."

"You don't say." Fargo gave them the benefit of the doubt—for the moment.

"We came up here a few years ago thinking to strike it rich, but we never did," Bucktooth revealed. "It's not right how some folks strike it and others don't. Life just ain't fair."

"I know a marmot who would agree if he was still breathing."

Bucktooth's brow puckered. "There you go again with the marmots. You're not addlepated, are you?"

"Not last I took stock, no."

"You sure don't look addlepated. But then, you never can tell about people by how they look."

Fargo was studying the others without being obvious. Two were smirking as if they shared a secret. The third gnawed nonstop on his lower lip. They were sloppy, this bunch. "I was thinking the same thing."

"How's that, mister?" Bucktooth asked while moving a step so he was between Fargo and his three friends.

"Nothing."

Bucktooth's brow lines deepened. "You sure do puzzle me. But I'd like to ask you a question, if that's all right."

"Asking is free."

Bucktooth pointed down the mountain at the line of riders and pack animals. "You're with them, I take it? By your buckskins, I'd say you must be their guide."

Fargo nodded.

Pleased at his deduction, Bucktooth grinned. "We've been watching awhile. They're still a ways off yet, so we can't be sure, but I'd swear that a couple of them are female."

Again Fargo nodded.

"Well, what do you know? There's not a heap of females in these parts. Yale's got some, and Spuzzum, maybe a few in

Boston Bar, and I don't know how many up to Lytton. But generally the menfolk outnumber the womenfolk ten to one."

Fargo didn't say anything. West of the Mississippi River that was normal. He shifted slightly to try to see what the three men behind Bucktooth were doing.

"Anyway, I figure there must be fifteen to twenty in your party. Is that about right?"

"More or less."

"They'll be a while getting here," Bucktooth said, more to himself than to Fargo. "So we have plenty of time."

"For what?"

"This." Bucktooth moved to one side.

Fargo found himself staring down the muzzles of several pistols. Pretending to be shocked, he said, "What are you up to?"

"See if you can guess," Bucktooth sarcastically prompted.

"You aim to rob us? Just the four of you?"

"We are good at it, if I say so my own self," Bucktooth boasted. "Two or three volleys and we'll drop most of your friends. The rest will panic and run around like chickens with their heads chopped off. They'll be easy. Then your horses and everything else you own will be ours."

Fargo couldn't get over how casual they were about it. "The British won't like it much."

"The Brits?" Bucktooth repeated, and laughed. "Their law ain't like our law, where we'd have a whole posse after us. Their law is one measly sheriff and maybe a helper or two. By the time he takes up our trail, we'll be on the coast."

"You've been doing this a while, I take it," Fargo stalled. He leaned forward so his holster was close to his right hand.

"Since fifty-nine," Bucktooth admitted. "It's too much work to go after gold the honest way, so we started taking it from those who didn't mind breaking their backs. We've been at it since."

"Honest work has one advantage."

"What, besides a sore back?"

"It doesn't get you hanged."

Bucktooth laughed. "Why sweat for it when it's there for the taking?" He put his hands on his hips. "You won't believe this, but I sort of like you. It's a shame we have to buck you out in gore like the rest."

One of the others asked, "Shouldn't we get to it?"

"And have them hear the shot below?" Bucktooth shook his head. "Use your head, Wiggins. We'll keep him here with us so when they come over that rise, they'll think we're peaceable. Let them get nice and close before we open up on them. They won't stand a prayer."

"You think of everything," Fargo said.

Bucktooth beamed at his friends. "Did you hear? Haven't I been saying that all along? You gents should put more trust in me."

"All except one thing," Fargo amended.

"Eh?" Bucktooth glanced up." I have this all thought out. Don't tell me I don't."

"You don't."

Bucktooth's features hardened. "Where did I make a mistake?"

"How do I explain this?" Fargo thoughtfully scratched his chin with his left hand while easing forward another inch so his right hand brushed his Colt. "Earlier I saw a marmot—"

"Oh Lord," Bucktooth interrupted. "Not the marmots again."

"It was snug and safe in its burrow until a griz came along, dug it out, and ate it."

"What does that have to do with me and my pards? We're not marmots, you dimwit."

"But you think that because you have me covered, you're as safe as that marmot thought he was. But the grizzly got in so close, there was nothing the marmot could do."

"You're no griz."

"But I'm close," Fargo said.

"So what?"

"You let me ride up, thinking I was like most anyone else. But you've made the same mistake that marmot made."

"Lordy, if I hear one more word about marmots, I'm liable to throw a fit. But I'll humor you. Is there a point to this?"

"That marmot didn't count on something coming along that was strong enough to dig it out of the ground. And you and your lunkhead pards didn't count on someone coming along who can draw and empty his six-gun in the time it takes you to blink."

"Oh, hell. You don't scare us none. We're not slouches ourselves," Bucktooth said smugly.

"It's the practice," Fargo said.

"The what?"

"More hours than you can count. More lead than would fill a Conestoga."

"Brag and more brag," Bucktooth said, but uncertainty tinged his tone and he glanced sharply at Fargo's holster. "Damn me. I should have taken that smoke wagon of yours right off."

"Yes, you should have."

One of the men covering Fargo gave a loud snort. "What the hell is this? If he so much as twitches, we'll put windows in his noggin. Just have him drop that lead chucker, and do it quick."

Bucktooth looked Fargo in the eyes and seemed to shiver slightly. "Damn me. They say it likely as not happens when you least expect it."

"What does?" one of the others asked.

"I didn't count on dying today," Bucktooth said rather sadly. And he went for his revolver.

Fargo drew and slammed off two shots, one for each of the men covering him. He shot them in the head so it only took one shot each, and even as they fell and the blasts had yet to echo off the surrounding slopes, he swiveled and shot the third man high in the sternum and swiveled again and pointed the Colt at Bucktooth, who only had his six-shooter half out.

Bucktooth froze, his face twisted in a sickly grimace. "Hell in a basket. You're no bluff." His throat bobbed. "What if I raise my hands and let you turn me over to the Brits?"

"How many others have you done this to?"

"Huh? What kind of question is that? I've never counted them. Thirty or forty, I reckon. What difference does it make?"

"None at all," Fargo said, and shot him between the eyes.

6

"You can't just go around shooting people whenever you feel like it," Edith Havard complained.

"It was either that or let them shoot you." Fargo had waited for the rest and now they were done with the burying and he was ready to ride on, but Edith insisted on bending his ear.

"Surely there was a better way to handle the situation."

"You're right. The best way would have been to let them shoot you and *then* shoot them."

"I'm only saying."

"You're bitching, lady, is what you're doing." Fargo wheeled and walked to the Ovaro. He was reaching for the saddle horn when Theodore Havard caught up with him.

"A word before you go, if you please, Mr. Fargo."

Fargo turned. Cosmo was with Theodore and Allen had followed them but stayed well back. "Your wife had it coming."

"Oh, it's not about her. I don't care what she does."

"We're wasting daylight."

"It's about Mr. Strath," Theodore said.

"I can shoot him, too."

"Honestly. Your attitude toward gunning down the populace is much too cavalier."

"When someone is asking for lead to the head, I oblige."

Theodore looked at Cosmo and then over his shoulder at his son. "We're straying from the point." He coughed for no reason. "Mr. Strath denies he tried to steal anything."

Fargo glanced at Cosmo, who would make a good poker

player; the butler's face was a blank slate. "What did you expect?"

"My son believes a mistake has been made. He doubts very much that Mr. Strath would resort to common thievery."

"I've said it before and I'll say it again. Your son is a jackass." The saddle creaked as Fargo swung on. He slid his other boot into the stirrup. "As your guide I have the final say. That was one of the things you agreed to, if you'll recollect."

"Yes, I remember. But what if you misjudged the man's intent?"

"Strath stays tied until we come across a sheriff or someone else who can take him off our hands."

"And that's your final word?"

Fargo reined around and tapped his spurs. If they could get over the pass before nightfall, tomorrow they would have easy going for the most part. Or as easy as the rugged British Columbian mountains ever got.

Tangling with the outlaws had reminded Fargo how dangerous this country was. He rode warily, his hand nearly always on his Colt.

The British were doing what they could but the few sheriffs weren't enough to handle the scores of killers and cutthroats. There was talk, Fargo had heard, of organizing some sort of police force, but nothing had come of it.

Fargo skirted a slope littered with deadfall. Later he had to skirt another covered with talus. The climb was steep. It was the middle of the afternoon when he reached the pass and climbed down to wait for the others. From up here he could see for miles and miles, breathtaking scenery the likes of which few ever beheld.

Many folks tended to forget there was more to the world than the town or city they lived in. Buildings and streets were all they saw each day. Seeped in civilization, their lives were the same, day in and day out, year after year.

That wasn't for Fargo. He preferred the wilds. The always

new. The always different. Give him the mountains and the prairies, the lakes and rivers and streams. He could only take civilization in small doses. Too much of it, and he felt suffocated and couldn't wait to head back into the wild.

Fargo sat on a boulder. The Havard party was a good ways below him. He reckoned it would take them an hour and a half to two hours to reach him. He squinted up at the sun. Plenty of daylight left. He would lead them through the pass and start down the other side of the mountain before night fell.

All things considered, it wasn't going badly. The business with Allen and Strath rankled but it was nothing to worry about. Bucktooth and company he rated as minor nuisances.

Fargo thought of Angeline, and stirred, low down. She had the kind of body a man dreamed about in the quiet hours of the night. He resented Cosmo for using that against him, but he didn't resent it too much. After all, he could have said no and told Theodore the truth.

Fargo stretched. He pushed his hat back on his head. He looked down at the ants winding slowly toward him and then sighed and turned to the Ovaro. He figured he might as well get some coffee going.

Two Indians were barely ten feet away.

Fargo stiffened and swooped his hand to his Colt. Then he saw that one of the Indians was a wrinkled old warrior with white hair and the other was a young maiden as shapely as Angeline Havard, with long raven hair and a doeskin dress decorated with beads and ribbons. They had high foreheads, high cheeks, and wide mouths. Both were armed with knives on their hips and the old warrior had a quiver and a bow slung across his back.

"It must be my day for running into people," Fargo muttered.

The woman was studying him intently. She smiled a bit uncertainly and said in English, "We are friendly."

"That's good to hear." Fargo returned her smile. "So am I.

43

Unless you're out to rob me or kill me, in which case I'm no marmot."

"Sorry?"

"Nothing," Fargo said. He introduced himself. "I take it you two are Knifes?"

"That is what your people call us. We call ourselves the Nlaka'pamux. I am Teit and this is my grandfather, Chelahit."

Fargo nodded at the old man and saw that he was staring off into space; his eyes were a filmy gray, not brown as they should be. "What's wrong with him?"

"My grandfather is blind."

Rising onto the toes of his boots, Fargo peered past them into the pass. "Where are the rest?"

"Sorry?"

"The other Nlaka'pamux." Fargo couldn't see her and her blind grandfather traipsing around by themselves.

"Thank you," Teit said.

"I didn't do anything."

"You called us by our name. Most whites cannot be bothered. To them we are the Knifes, whether we want to be or not." Teit smiled. "And there are no others. Grandfather and I are alone."

"That's dangerous."

"Thank you," Teit said again.

"What the hell for?"

"For saying that. You must have a good heart for a white man. I am well pleased."

Fargo's interest perked. But he exercised caution and took a few steps to the right so he could see to the far end of the pass and confirm her claim. The pass was empty. "What are you doing way up here by yourselves?"

"Long ago my grandfather's brother took a Nicola woman for his wife and went to live with them. My grandfather wanted to see his brother one more time before he passes to

44

the other side, so I took him for a visit. We are on our way back to our own people."

The Nicola, Fargo knew, were a tribe to the south. "Then you're on your way north, the same as me."

"We heard you come up the mountain and hid. I have watched you to be sure you are friendly."

"What made you decide I am?"

"I can tell," Teit said. "Early this morning four white men came down the trail and we hid from them, too. They were men with bad hearts."

"Bucktooth and his pards."

"Sorry?" Teit said yet again.

"You were right. They had bad hearts."

"Had?"

"I don't like having guns pointed at me."

Teit held her grandfather's hand, brought him to the boulder, and in her own tongue bade him sit.

"Does Chelahit speak the white tongue?"

"No. He is not fond of white men. He says whites want to own the world and that is wrong, so he will have nothing to do with them."

"You speak it well," Fargo complimented her. "Did a Catholic missionary teach you?" Priests had been active in the region in recent years.

"Father Fouquet, yes. A kind man. A good man. I learned from him, and from others. I learned well, yes?"

"You speak it better than me."

"I try hard to say it well," Teit said. "I also speak some French and the tongues of two tribes besides my own."

Fargo fished for information by remarking, "You're smart as well as good-looking. There must be a warrior somewhere lucky to call you his wife."

"I am too busy taking care of grandfather and my father and mother to think of a husband." Teit sighed. "My parents had me late in life. My father broke his leg in a fall five winters ago and cannot get around as he used to."

"I'm sorry to hear that," Fargo said to be polite.

"And you? Is there a woman you call your own?"

"I like all women. Tall, short. Blondes, redheads, brunettes." Fargo paused for effect. "White. Red."

"And women like you, I suspect. You are very handsome for a white man. It is your eyes. Looking into them is like looking into a lake."

Fargo hooked his thumbs in his belt. "Tell you what. Since you're heading in the same direction we are, you're welcome to join us, if you'd like."

"You can speak for all the whites below?" Teit asked with a sweep of her arm at the riders.

"They're not like the badmen you saw. I'm their guide. The man in charge is called Havard. He's up here searching for his son."

Teit gave a slight start. "Havard, you say?"

"You've heard the name before?"

"I do not think so."

"Theordore Havard, his wife, Edith, and their son and daughter are looking for the other son, Kenneth. Have you run across him anywhere?"

"No."

Fargo was willing to bet every dollar in his poke she was lying. ""He's lived in Fraser Canyon the past few years, working a gold claim."

"We do not go into the canyon often," Teit told him.

Now Fargo was doubly certain. Fraser Canyon was at the heart of Knife territory. Only small parts of it were under white control. The rest were roamed by the Knifes. "So you've never been to Boston Bar or Lytton?"

"A few times," she admitted.

Fargo let it drop, for now. He went to the Ovaro, groped in a saddlebag, and brought out a bundle of pemmican wrapped in a square of rabbit fur. He opened the hide and offered some to them.

"You are very kind," Teit said as she picked a piece for her grandfather and another for herself.

"You're welcome to more if you want."

Tentatively, almost shyly, Teit selected two more. She avoided looking at him. Sitting next to her grandfather, she slowly chewed. "Thank you. This is. . . . how do you say?. . . . delicious?"

"I think so, too." Fargo liked pemmican a lot better than jerky. It consisted of berries mixed with meat and fat. He wrapped the bundle and replaced it in his saddlebag.

They ate in silence. Several times Teit glanced at Fargo as if she was going to say something. Chelahit finished his pemmican and carefully eased to the ground with his back to the boulder. He said something to Teit.

"My grandfather says he is sleepy. He will rest while we wait for your friends," she translated.

Fargo moved a few yards down the slope and leaned against a fir, his arm crossed over his chest. The panorama of uplands spread before him to the far horizon. Several peaks were capped with ivory even at that time of year. Below the snow, phalanxes of evergreens grew in their many diversities. A pair of ravens cawed and flapped, the throb of their wings like the beat of a pulse in the rarefied air.

"Beautiful, is it not?" Teit asked as she sat next to him.

"The only thing more beautiful is a woman's naked body." Fargo smiled as he said it but she still blinked.

"Are you always this forward?"

"A popular question of late," Fargo admitted. "But you should be used to it, as pretty as you are."

"Used to what? Most men I know do not talk about female bodies, naked or otherwise."

Fargo thought she had risen to the bait but she immediately changed the subject.

"This Kenneth Havard. His family is sure he was in Fraser Canyon?"

"They got regular letters from him and then the letters stopped. His claim was near Boston Bar."

"I see." Teit hesitated. "It could be they have come all this way for nothing. It could be he is dead."

"Do you know something I don't?"

"No. I was just saying. Many of the whites who came to our country found only death." Teit put a hand on his arm. "It is worth keeping in mind. You have been kind to us, and I would not want you to be one of them."

Was that a warning or a threat? Fargo wondered.

7

Fargo figured someone would object. He didn't figure on the entire Havard family, and Cosmo, coming up to him with spite in their eyes. Edith fired the first shot.

"What is this nonsense about you wanting that old Indian and that squaw to join us?"

"Only as far as Fraser Canyon."

"Why would you even want to do such a thing?" Theodore demanded. "They're Indians, after all."

Fargo had three reasons. He wanted to help Teit and her grandfather get back safely. He wanted to do it because he was convinced Teit knew something about Kenneth Havard. And he wanted to do it because he wanted to get up her dress. He mentioned only the first reason.

Theodore harrumped. "Are you sane? These are red savages we're talking about. We will need protection from *them*."

"From a blind man and his grandaughter?"

Edith thrust a finger at him. "They're heathens, and I for one do not associate with heathens."

Allen had been quiet but now he said in his most condescending tone, "Why all this bickering? It's not as if our guide has a choice. He works for us. He'll do what we want him to do. That's all there is to it."

"I work for your father," Fargo set him straight. "I'll hash this out with him. Keep your braying to yourself."

The allusion to a jackass caused red to creep from Allen's pale throat to his pale forehead.

"That will be quite enough," Theodore interceded. "We're serious, Fargo. I will not have savages in my party, and that's final."

"Then you don't have me, either."

Allen quickly said, "We don't need him, Father. We're only a day out of Fraser Canyon. We can find Boston Bar by ourselves."

"Be my guest," Fargo said.

At that juncture Cosmo cleared his throat. "Permit me, Theodore, to add my thoughts."

"Of course."

"It's true we are near enough to the canyon that we can probably find it on our own, and thus true that we don't need Mr. Fargo's services as a guide, per se. But we *do* need his experience. Remember those four men who were out to kill and rob us?"

"As always, you make an excellent point," Theodore praised him.

"There's more to consider." Cosmo looked at each of the Havards. "It's my understanding Indians are often grateful for a kindness rendered. By helping this girl and her grandfather, we show her people that we are friendly. And surely it's to our benefit to be in the good graces of the Knife Indians, given the trouble they have caused in the past."

"Another excellent point," Theodore agreed.

"I don't agree," Edith said bitterly.

"But, my dear, they are less likely to attack if we've done them a favor. By helping these two, we reap goodwill."

"Exactly my point," Cosmo said.

Fargo had to hand it him; the man didn't miss much. He noticed that Angeline was not taking part and smiled at her. She smiled back.

"I still think it's a mistake," Edith stubbornly insisted.

"I'm with mother," Allen declared.

McKern and several others were listening, and McKern

chose that moment to clear his throat. "Have you ever fought redskins, Mrs. Havard?"

"Of course not. I've spent my entire life in cities in cultured, mannered society. *White* society."

"That's nice. But out here culture doesn't count for much. If we get the Knifes mad at us, we could have a rain of arrows come out of nowhere. Or maybe they'll sneak into our camp some night and slit a few of our throats from ear to ear. They've done it before."

Theodore rubbed his chin. "Very well. It's worth it to get into the good graces of the savages. The woman and her grandfather may stay." He turned to Fargo. "But make them understand they are not to bother us. They're not to beg for food or money or any of that. We'll show them whites can be as kind as anyone, within certain limits."

And that was that.

Teit thanked Fargo when he brought the news. He took them to near the rear of the line, just ahead of Rohan and the pack animals. Rohan was picking lice from his clothes.

"Mind? Why would I mind? I've got nothing against Injuns. Down to Texas I had a friend name of Blue Dog. He was half Comanch, but him and me got along just fine."

Fargo's estimation of the Texan rose a notch. "Keep an eye on them and let me know if anyone gives them trouble. Mrs. Havard and Allen don't like the idea."

"Now there's a pair. A shrew and a weasel," Rohan scoffed. "The airs that Allen puts on, I'd love to take a hatchet to his head. Anything that gets him mad, I'm for."

Fargo led them through the pass and down the other side. Mostly bare slopes made their going easy the first mile. Then they came to the thick timber.

Fargo called a halt at the tree line.

As usual, Cosmo took charge. The tents were put up. Wood was chopped. Fires were kindled. Rohan saw to the horses.

His Henry in hand, Fargo went to where the maiden and

her grandfather were sat quietly by themselves. "I'll see to it you get some food, and later we can talk if you want."

"About what?" Teit asked.

"Your people. I like to learn about tribes I've never met." Fargo hoped in the bargain to learn about Kenneth Havard.

Teit gazed out over the vast expanse of peaks and darkening woods. "This land is our land. We have lived here for more winters than anyone can count. We do not like that the whites have come. We especially do not like that the whites act as if the land is theirs."

"Not all whites. You mentioned a priest you liked."

"One of only a few white men with good hearts. If more were like Father Fouquet and K—" Teit caught herself and stopped.

Fargo would swear she was about to say "Kenneth" but he pretended not to notice. "Maybe before long you'll add me to that list."

Teit smiled. "I would like to."

On that promising note Fargo went to the fire nearest the tents. The Havards were not out yet. Their nightly ritual included washing up for supper. Edith, in particular, had a fit if so much as a mote of dust besmirched her powdered skin.

Cosmo had put coffee on. Squatting, Fargo filled his tin cup. The aroma of simmering stew made his mouth water. "You should be a cook." The man was a wizard with pots and pans.

Without looking up from the potatoes he was chopping, Cosmo chuckled. "It is part of my job. I have no passion for it, and a person should always devote him- or herself to something they are passionate about."

Fargo thought of his love of the wild places, and of women. "I guess I never looked at it that way."

About to add the potatoes pieces to the pot, Cosmo commented, "That's one of the traits I admire about you."

"*You* admire *me*?"

"Why do you sound so surprised? I like to think of myself as intelligent, and intelligence appreciates quality, wherever it may be found."

"You sure like big words."

Cosmo grinned. "We all have our pretensions."

"What the hell does that mean?"

"Surely you have met people who pretend they are something they are not? The put on a show, and the show is their life. I'll use Allen as an example. He pretends to be a loving, devoted son. But the truth is, he's a spoiled brat who can't wait for Theodore and Mrs. Havard to die so he can lay claim to his share of their inheritance." Cosmo began chopping carrots. "Or let's take a certain young lady you are interested in. She puts on a show of being shy and inhibited. But the truth be known, she has had several, shall we say, dalliances in recent years. She isn't the complete innocent she lets on."

"Why are you telling me this?"

Cosmo's smile was oil mixed in water. "You asked me about pretensions, remember? Is there anything else you would like to know?"

Fargo was about to say no, but actually there was. "How close are Allen and Kenneth?"

"Not close at all. There's the age difference, for one thing. Kenneth always loved the outdoors. Allen isn't happy unless he has a roof over his head. Kenneth could take care of himself. Allen is a mother's boy. Need I go on?"

"I get the idea."

Jut then the flap to Angeline's tent parted and out she strolled in a dress more fit for the San Francisco theater than the mountains of British Columbia. It clung to her ripe body in all the right places and was cut scandalously low in front to accent her cleavage. Fargo whistled softly.

Her hands clasped behind her back so that her bosom thrust against her dress, Angeline ignored his whistle and asked Cosmo, "How long until supper is ready?"

"Half an hour, young miss, perhaps a bit longer. Your father mentioned he's famished and I want the food to be just right."

"Plenty of time." Angeline swiveled toward Fargo. "I can stand to stretch my legs after being in the saddle all day. Care to go for a walk?"

"I suppose I can force myself."

Cosmo made a sound that was part chuckle and part cough. "By all means, enjoy yourselves. I will—what is the expression?—oh, yes, I'll give a holler when the meal is ready."

"You're a card, Cosmo," Angeline told him.

"So long as it's the queen of hearts. Now you be careful out there. Watch out for insects and snakes and whatever else might bite you."

Perfume wreathed Fargo like an invisible cloud. He admired how Angeline's dress molded to the sweep of her thighs, and he twitched below his belt.

"I must admit I've been looking forward to this," Angeline said. "Going for a walk, I mean. But it wouldn't be safe to go alone. That's why I asked you to come."

Fargo refrained from pointing out that she wasn't all that safe with him along. "You learned your lesson from that bear."

"I learned my lesson from being female. You have no idea what it's like for a woman. The constant advances. The gropes. The hungry looks."

They entered the forest. Starlight relieved the black of night, enough for Fargo to see the white of her teeth when she smiled.

"I had my nerve calling you 'bold and brazen,' didn't I?"

Never one to waste an opportunity, Fargo placed his hands on her hips and stopped. "What did you have in mind?"

"Oh my." Angeline gave a nervous laugh and glanced at the camp. "We haven't gone far enough for that yet."

Fargo motioned. "Lead on."

Angeline wasn't satisfied until the trees screened her from the campfires. In a clear space between a pair of tall spruce trees, she halted and announced, "Right here is nice."

The darkness was an inky cocoon, the wilderness unusually still. But it was early yet. Soon the meat eaters would be on the prowl, filling the night with their howls and roars and screeches.

"You sure are," Fargo said. Once again he placed his hands on the swell of her hips, and pulled her to him. Her breath fluttered on his cheek. She had the aspect of a frightened doe about to bolt.

"My, you work fast."

"Half an hour isn't a lot of time unless you like it hard and fast." Fargo liked it any way he could get it, but some women weren't fond of quick. They preferred to take their time and to kiss and fondle. Some women even had to be courted first, with a meal and flowers and a night on the town. Then there were those, thankfully few, who demanded the man get down on his knees and beg for it.

Fargo had never begged for it in his life, and he would be damned if he ever would. Either the woman wanted to or she didn't, and if she didn't, he moved to greener pastures. It was that simple.

"I don't mind hard and fast—"

"Good." Fargo reached for her breasts.

"—provided we build up to it easy and slow."

Fargo cocked his head. Only a woman would say something like that. "Whatever you want." He cupped her breasts and squeezed.

"Ohhh!" Angeline arched her back, her luscious lips parted. "You won't hurt me, will you?"

"Does this hurt?" Fargo asked, and pinched her nipples. He covered her lips with his and she gasped into his mouth. He reached behind her and cupped her bottom and kneaded it while slowly easing her back against a spruce. Angeline moaned. The feel of her silken dress and the hint of delights under it were intoxicating. Their kiss went on and on, until finally he broke it.

"Marvelous," Angeline breathed huskily, her eyes hooded with burning desire.

"I'm just getting started." Fargo ran his hand from her knee to the junction of her thighs. She was warm to the touch and growing warmer. He went to hike up her dress so he could slide his hand underneath when she stiffened and pushed against his shoulders.

"No!"

"What the matter?" Fargo hadn't taken her for a tease.

Angeline put her lips to his ear and whispered in fear, "We're being watched!"

8

Fargo spun in the direction she was pointing.

Deep in the gloom was a dusky silhouette. The shape was human—of that there was no doubt.

"Is it one of our party?" Angeline anxiously whispered.

"Stay here." Fargo moved toward the silhouette, his hand on his Colt. He strained to make out details. Suddenly he realized a hand was clinging to the back of his shirt. "I told you to stay where you were."

"Nothing doing. If it's not one of ours, it could be a hostile or an outlaw or God knows what."

Fargo let her cling. He took a few more steps, and the shape was gone. One instant it was there; the next it wasn't.

"Where did it get to?" Angeline asked.

"Hush." Fargo suspected the person had gone to ground. He cautiously advanced until he was about where the shape had been. No one was there. He bent but it was too dark to read prints, if there even were any.

"That was scary."

"'Hush' means 'hush.'" Fargo stood and listened. The wind in the trees was all he heard.

Angeline glued herself to his side and glanced nervously about. "Is it safe for us to be out here?"

For an answer, Fargo cupped her bottom.

"What do you think you're doing?"

"Taking up where we left off." Fargo went to kiss her but she stepped back.

"After what we just saw? How can you even think I would want to? Be sensible."

"Whoever it was ran off. We're fine." Fargo reached for her again.

"'No' means 'no,'" Angeline mimicked him, and pushed against his chest. "Take me back. I couldn't now. I'm sorry. That's just how it is."

Fargo bit off a few choice words. Taking her hand, he made for camp. When the campfires appeared, she stopped pressing against him.

"We must tell Father. Maybe you should organize a search and take torches and scour the woods."

"If whoever it was is still out here, they'd see us."

"It's worth a try."

"The men are tired and hungry. I'll look myself come morning. If there are tracks I'll find them."

"Why must you be so pigheaded?"

"Why must you be a nag?"

That shut Angeline up. She didn't say another word until they emerged from the forest. "Thank you for the walk," she declared, and headed for her tent.

Fargo sighed and went to a fire where McKern and Rohan and others were hunkered. He sank down next to the old man. "Seen anyone leave camp in the past twenty minutes?"

"Besides you and the pretty filly? No, I did not."

Rohan said, "We figured you were showing her all about the birds and the bees. But you weren't gone long enough for that."

"Show some respect," McKern said.

"I wasn't poking fun. It's what comes natural. Horses do it all the time. The other night that stallion of his took an interest in one of the mares, but she wasn't in the mood." Rohan chuckled. "I would have loved to watch them go at it. Ever seen how big a stallion gets?"

"You are a strange man."

Fargo left them and went to the cook fire. He always ate with the Havards. Ordinarily he didn't mind because it gave him a chance to talk to Angeline. But tonight she was quiet and withdrawn. No one seemed to notice. Theodore mentioned how glad he was that their journey would soon be over. Edith said as how she couldn't wait to see Kenneth again.

"If he's still alive," Allen remarked.

"I won't have talk like that. He has to be."

"No one ever has to be anything, Mother. Certainly I want to find Kenneth alive and well. But we must be realistic. This country is overrun with savages and badmen. Have you forgotten those men we buried today?"

Edith shot a sharp look at Fargo. "I haven't forgotten anything, thank you very much. But I won't have you suggesting the unthinkable."

Theodore said curtly, "That's enough, both of you. And, Allen, so what if this country is hard on men? Your brother can take care of himself. Spare your mother her feelings, if you don't mind, and even if you do."

"Yes, Father."

Cosmo, who was filling a bowl with soup, drily commented, "At times like this, I wonder why I never had a family of my own."

"Don't start," Theodore said.

Fargo tried to catch Angeline's eye but she deliberately avoided looking at him. He was about done with his stew when Theodore had a question.

"How long can you stay with us? I contracted for you to bring us here, but that was all. And I'd like for you to stick around and help us if it turns out Kenneth isn't at Boston Bar, as we hope."

Fargo hadn't given the matter any thought, and said so.

"I'll pay you however much you would like."

Allen stopped eating and scowled. "Honestly, Father, it's a wonder we have any money left, the way you squander it."

"It's *my* money and I'll do with it as I please. Don't worry. I'll leave you enough of an inheritance to get by."

"I expect a third, nothing less."

Theodore started to rise but Cosmo glanced at him and shook his head and Theodore sank back down. "You'll take what I leave you and be glad I left you anything. And for your information, it won't be a third. There's your mother and you and your brother and sister. Plus a few others."

"By a few you mean Cosmo."

"I beg your pardon?"

Edith said, "Allen, don't."

"It's time it came out, Mother," Allen responded. "So tell us, Father. Are you leaving a sizable amount to your precious friend?"

Now Theodore did rise, and he was shaking with barely contained fury. "I will thank you not to talk about him that way. He has been of more worth to me than you could ever hope to be."

Allen stood, too. "Of course he has. But then, I'm only your son."

Angeline finally broke her silence. "Let it drop. You do none of us any favors."

To Fargo's surprise, Allen glanced at him.

"Do you hear this? Perish forbid we should air our dark family secrets in public. But you see how it is, don't you? How a son can rate so low in his own father's affections?"

Theodore balled his bony fists. "That has nothing to do with Cosmo and everything to do with you and your attitude. You are insolent. You are lazy. You talk about squandering? Any money I leave you, you'll waste on the nightlife you love so much."

"Culture is costly, Father. But very well. As usual, everyone is against me. If you'll excuse me, it's been a trying day and I think I'll retire." Allen wheeled and strode to his tent. At the flap he looked back. "A last thought, Father. It could be I'm more loyal than any of them. Did you ever think of that?

I've kept your secret all these years, haven't I?" The flap closed behind him.

"I never," Edith said.

Theodore sadly bowed his head. "I've given him everything and this is how he repays me."

"Pay him no mind, Father," Angeline said. "He delights in upsetting people. It's in his nature."

Cosmo cleared his throat. "Might I suggest we forget his ill manners and enjoy our meal?"

Fargo had had enough. He refilled his tin and walked off. The camp was quiet save for low voices and an occasional laugh. Overhead, myriad stars gleamed. He bent his head back and was admiring them when someone spoke almost at his feet.

"Be careful or you will step on us."

Teit and Chelahit were huddled next to each other, nearly invisible in the dark.

It occurred to Fargo that he hadn't laid eyes on them since the sun went down. "What are you two doing over here by yourselves?"

"It is best."

Fargo squatted. "Best how?" He went to take a sip of coffee and her grandfather sniffed.

Teit nodded toward the campfires. "They do not want our company. McKern is nice to us. And the horse man, Rohan. But the rest look at us with suspicious eyes."

"There's no shortage of stupid in this world." Fargo held his cup closer to them and her grandfather sniffed again. "Have you two had a bite to eat or anything to drink?"

"I did not want to impose."

"Hell." Fargo rose and walked to the cook fire. He filled two bowls, put wooden spoons in them, and carried the bowls back. "Here. And don't give me any bull about not being hungry."

"We have no money to pay you."

"Who asked for any?" Fargo placed a bowl in her lap and

touched the other bowl to her grandfather's chest. The old man went to take it but hesitated, turned his head to her, and said something in their own tongue. She answered, then looked up.

"Why are you being so kind to us?"

"You're hungry. Eat." Fargo touched the bowl to the grandfather again and this time he took it. He returned to the fire and filled two cups with coffee. As he was about to walk off, Edith Havard cleared her throat.

"Are those for that squaw and her grandfather?"

Fargo nodded.

"You have your gall. You might ask before you share our food. We paid for the supplies, not you."

"You'd deny them this little bit?"

"They're Indians," Edith said, as if that were cause enough. "And you're the one who invited them along. You should have thought of their stomachs sooner and shot game for them to eat."

"Now, Mother," Angeline said.

"Don't take that tone with me, young lady. You father can sit here mute if he wants, but I will speak my mind. It frustrates me no end, the liberties our guide takes."

Fargo made no attempt to hide his contempt. "I have to hand it to you, lady."

"Hand what?"

"I've met some bitches in my time, but you are at the top of the heap." Fargo left her fuming. People like her were the reason he couldn't stand civilization for more than short spells. He crossed to the Nlaka'pamux.

"Thank you. My grandfather is very fond of coffee." Tiet paused. "I saw you arguing with the white woman with eyes of flint. Did she not want you to bring these to us?"

"Who cares what she wants?" Fargo sat cross-legged and propped his elbows on his knees. "We need to talk, you and me."

"We do?"

"Kenneth Havard." Fargo held up a hand. "Don't deny you've heard of him. I saw your face earlier. What do you know that I should know?"

Holding the cup in both hands, Teit blew on the coffee to cool it. "I am sorry. If I tell you and his family finds out, there will be much trouble."

"Is he dead?"

"Please."

"It's easy to answer. Yes or no. If it's yes, where's the grave? I'll take them there and they can be on their way."

Teit lowered the cup and bowed her head. "You do not understand."

"I'm trying." Fargo was glad to be proven right but puzzled by her reluctance to say. Then it hit him. "Are the Nlaka'pamux involved? Did he do something to anger them and pay with his life?"

"My people would never harm Kenneth Havard. His heart, like yours, is good."

"Is? Then he *is* still alive?"

"I never said that."

Fargo wouldn't let it drop. "But where did he get to? And why did he stop writing his folks?"

"He has his rea—" Teit stopped. "Oh, you are terrible."

Teit put down the cup and grasped Chelahit's hand. "My grandfather and I should go. If I stay I might say things I shouldn't, and upset people I care for dearly."

"No. Wait." Fargo put his hand on her leg, above the knee. So long as they stayed, he stood a chance of prying the truth out of her. "I won't bring it up again if you don't want me to talk about him."

"I don't."

"All right. Not another word." For a while, anyway, Fargo told himself.

Teit's eyes were limpid pools. "But there is something I do want. Something I would like very much."

"Name it."

"I saw you walk off with the white girl. I would like for you to walk off with me."

Fargo was instantly wary. "Just the two of us? Why? What do you have in mind?"

Teit grinned. "I should think you could guess." She held out her hand for him to take. "I want you to make love to me."

9

Skye Fargo liked women as much as whiskey and poker. Their bodies gave him more pleasure than just about anything. But they also did things that left him scratching his head. They were hard to figure out. Not other men. Men thought a certain way and did things a certain way, and reading them was easy. The same with wild animals. Once you knew an animal's habits, you knew the animal. But women didn't think as men did and things they did often made no sense.

Ask most any man and he would tell you that women were a delight but they were *strange*.

Fargo liked the idea of going off in the woods with Teit. She had a nice body. But the offer came so unexpectedly that he was suspicious. It struck him as peculiar that she wanted to go off with him when she had not shown any sign of being interested in him earlier.

Still, it *was* sex she was talking about, so Fargo heard himself say, "Lead the way."

Teit spoke softly into her grandfather's ear. He grunted and said a few sharp words. She said to Fargo, "Come. Let us go."

They entered the woods, Teit in the lead.

"What was that about?"

"I told him to stay where he is, that I was going for a walk with you and I would not be very long."

"He doesn't mind you being with a white man?"

"He would rather I was with one of my people than with you, yes."

"Why *are* you doing this?"

"If I tell you, you will think I am silly."

"Try me."

To the north wolves howled. The wind gusted, stirring the trees.

Teit was slow to answer. Finally she said, "Very well. But I must make clear it was not my intent to—What is the word? Oh, yes. It was not my intent to spy on you."

"When?"

"I saw you and the white girl."

Fargo remembered the silhouette off through the trees. "That was you? What were you doing out there by yourself?"

"What do you think?"

"Oh." Fargo chuckled. "But that still doesn't explain why you're going off with me now."

"It excited me."

They had gone far enough. Stopping, Fargo pulled her to him and slid his arms around her waist from behind. She didn't resist. He nuzzled her neck and nipped her earlobe. "You'll be a lot more excited before I'm done."

"I hope so. It has been a long while since a man has interested me as you do. And never before a white man."

"I'm flattered."

"It is not good for white and red to mix. Not here, anyway. There has been too much hate, too much spilled blood. Not long ago a white man and a woman from my village fell in love. Other whites were mean to them. Very mean. It made the woman sad and the man very mad."

"Enough talk." Fargo turned her head and kissed her. Her lips were warm and soft. She yielded eagerly. She wasn't lying about being excited.

Fargo ran a hand from her waist to her breasts and cupped one. It was round and full, the nipple erect. He gave the other his attention and soon she was panting and grinding her bottom against him. His manhood became an iron rod.

Fargo didn't like that her hair was in braids. He preferred it loose so he could run his hands through it and pull it. He took hold of one and bent her head back so he could lather her throat. She cooed like a dove, her fingers exploring him as he was exploring her.

At length Fargo eased Teit to the ground. He stretched out beside her and hiked up her dress until it was up around her hips. Her legs were as nice as the rest of her, her thighs soft and pliant. He caressed them with one hand while his other was up under her dress, kneading her breasts. They filled his palm as if made for that purpose. Each time he pinched a nipple, she groaned.

The whole time, Fargo listened for sounds that would warn him they weren't alone. The stillness troubled him. It might mean a bear or a big cat was in the area. Or it could just be the presence of their camp. Most animals wanted nothing to do with man, the great destroyer of all that lived.

Teit took Fargo's hat off and did to his hair what he had wanted to do to her. She pulled so hard, he thought she would tear his hair out by the roots. She also bit his lip and raked her nails.

"Like it a little rough, do you?" Fargo said, and squeezed a breast fit to rip it off.

Teit arched her back and gasped and dug her nails in deeper. "Yes! Oh yes!"

Fargo was in no hurry. They had been at it a while when she put her lips to his ear.

"Do not take all night. I must not leave my grandfather alone very long. Some of the men with you look at us with eyes of hate."

"Whatever you want."

Spreading her legs, Fargo knelt between them. He undid his belt and slid his pants down. His member was a flagpole. She cupped him, and his throat constricted.

"My, you are big."

Fargo touched her. "My, you are wet." He ran the tip of his manhood along her moist slit, inserted it, and rammed up into her.

Teit's eyes grew wide, her mouth an oval. "Oh! Oh! You fill me."

Fargo held himself still, savoring the sensation. Then, placing his hands on her hips, he rocked on his knees. She locked her ankles behind him and met each thrust with a grind of her pelvis. Her lips found his and stayed there. He went faster and she went faster and he thrust harder and she ground harder until they attained the peak. She crested first, biting his shoulder and going into a paroxysm of release. His own soon followed, and together they coasted to a stop and lay covered with sweat and breathing heavily.

A lassitude came over him and Fargo closed his eyes. He would have dozed off if she hadn't poked him.

"We must go back. My grandfather."

Reluctantly, Fargo rolled off her. He got his pants up and his belt buckled and found his hat. She was already on her feet and had smoothed her dress, and to look at her you wouldn't think that not two minutes ago she had been in the throes of passion.

"You are a turtle," Teit said.

"Women," Fargo muttered, and rose. She started off and he caught up, saying, "I doubt anything has happened to him."

"If it did I could never live with myself for leaving him alone, even for a short while."

"He'll be fine. He'd have yelled if anything was wrong."

"I am still uneasy."

Fargo was looking at her and not at the woods around them. Out of the corner of his eye he caught swift movement and the glint of cold steel, and barely twisted aside in time. As it was, the blade bit into his sleeve and his skin and drew blood. Shoving Teit out of the way, he whirled to confront his attacker, who had crouched and was holding two knives down low. "You."

"Me," Strath said.

Fargo went for his Colt. Strath was expecting it and a knife flashed. Fargo had to jerk his hand away or lose fingers. He sprang back and again grabbed for the Colt, but Strath came after him, swinging one knife at Fargo's hand and the other at his throat. Sidestepping, Fargo avoided both blades. Strath instantly pivoted toward him and he seized both of Strath's wrists.

"Damn you!" Strath hissed.

Fargo was bigger, heavier. He sought to force Strath to the ground, but Strath was wiry and quick, and he shifted and twisted, thwarting him. They spun back and forth and around and around in a macabre dance of death. Strath aimed a kick at Fargo's groin, but Fargo turned enough that his outer thigh took the blow.

Strath continued to hiss and to snarl like some animal. A feral gleam lit his eyes. He was out to kill, whatever it took.

Fargo had lost track of Teit. He hoped she had the good sense to stay out of it. Another kick nearly caught him in the knee. Strath rammed his forehead at Fargo's mouth. He turned his head just in time, but pain exploded in his ear. In pulsing anger, Fargo slammed him against a tree.

Strath swore and arced a knee into Fargo's ribs. Fargo did likewise. But as he raised his leg, Strath hooked a foot around the other one and pushed. Down Fargo fell, pulling Strath after him. They wound up with Fargo on his back and Strath on his chest, grinning from ear to ear.

"I have you now, you son of a bitch." Strath drove both knives down, seeking to bury them.

A razor tip was inches from Fargo's neck. Fargo locked his elbow, stopping its descent. The other blade was close to his chest; Strath was trying to stick him in the heart.

Fargo bucked upward. Strath tumbled to one side and

jerked a wrist free. Before he could stab, Fargo kicked him in the chest.

Strath went rolling.

Fargo heaved to his feet and streaked the Colt from his holster. He had Strath now. He thumbed back the hammer as Strath turned toward him, and Strath froze.

"Go ahead, damn you."

Fargo wanted to. God, how he wanted to. But he didn't squeeze the trigger. The last he saw, Strath had been tied and under guard. Someone had to help Strath get free, and he wanted to know who that someone was. "Drop those pig stickers of yours and tell me how you got free."

"Go to hell."

"If that's how you want it, I'll send you there ahead of me." Fargo waited, giving Strath time to mull the benefits of breathing over being worm food.

"You won't shoot?"

"I give you my word."

Swearing luridly, Strath nonetheless let his knives fall, held his arms out from his sides, and took a step back. "There. Happy now?"

"I will be when you tell me. Wilson was guarding you, wasn't he?"

"He didn't do a very good job. He's lying back at camp with his head half caved in."

"Who did the caving? You or someone else?"

"I'll never tell."

"You will or you'll take lead."

"You'd shoot an unarmed man? You don't strike me as the type. I'd do it but you never would."

"It was Allen Havard, wasn't it?"

Strath laughed in contempt. "As much as I'm being paid, do you really think I'll say?"

Fargo was sure it was one of the Havards. It had to be someone with money. Allen was the logical suspect. "Turn

70

around and start walking." Once he got them to camp, he might be able to trick Allen into giving himself away.

"Sure, sure, big man."

"Keep those hands where I can see them."

"Anything you want."

This whole time, Teit had stayed well back with her hand on the hilt of her knife. Now, at a glance from Fargo, she came to his side.

"That man has a bad heart."

Strath heard her and chortled. "Squaw, you don't know the half of it. Some of the things I've done would give you goose-flesh." He leered at her and lecherously rimmed his slit of a mouth with his tongue. "Just say the word and I'll do things to you that will curl your toes."

"I have just had my toes curled, thank you, and do not need them curled again."

"Did you hear that, big man? She paid you a compliment." Strath threw back his head and opened his mouth to laugh.

That was when a shot boomed, just one, a rifle off in the dark evergreens. The slug went through Strath's open mouth, cored his cranium, and erupted out the rear of his skull, spattering gore and blood and hair. Dead on his feet, the killer did a slow pirouette to the ground.

Fargo was in a crouch. He yanked Teit down and sought some sign of the shooter. But there wasn't so much as a wisp of gun smoke. He waited, unwilling to show himself and take a bullet.

From the direction of the camp, shouts rose.

Teit had drawn her knife. "Who do you think it is?" she whispered. "The one they call Allen?"

"That would be my guess." But something about it bothered Fargo—something he couldn't put a mental finger on.

"Listen."

There were more yells and the crackle of brush. Fargo heard his name called.

"They should not see us together," Teit said.

"What difference does it make?" Fargo asked. When she didn't answer, he turned—she was gone.

Then McKern and Rohan and Cosmo and several others were rushing out of the night and still calling his name, and Fargo rose and answered. Within seconds they had converged.

"Is that Strath?" McKern asked with a nod at the form on its face in the dirt.

Fargo nodded.

"Did you shoot him? I thought it was a rifle I heard."

"It was."

"But all you have is your Colt. What the hell is going on?"

"I wish I knew."

10

No one knew how Strath had gotten free. That he had help was obvious; Wilson, the man who was guarding him, had been hit from behind with a rock. Wilson had a deep gash but he would live. Fargo made Wilson go to where he had been sitting when he was hit.

Wilson grumpily complied, complaining, "I'd like to go lie down. My head hurts worse than any pain I ever had."

"Show me."

Wilson pointed at where Strath had been lying on his side, away from the fire, and then at where he had been sitting.

"Your back wasn't to the woods," Fargo noticed.

"Huh? No, I reckon it wasn't. My back was to the tents. Why? Does it matter?"

"It could and it couldn't." Fargo went to the fire and poured another cup a cup of coffee. Most everyone had gone back to sleep. Strath was wrapped in a blanket and would be buried first thing in the morning.

Fargo was raising the cup when he sensed her come up next to him.

"What were you doing out in the woods with that Indian girl?"

"None of your business."

Angeline was bundled in a thick robe that covered her from her feet to her neck. "I would very much like to know."

"We went for a stroll."

"I wasn't born yesterday, Skye Fargo. And I feel I have the right to ask after you and I—" Angeline stopped.

"You and I what? We were interrupted, remember? And even if we had, that doesn't give you a claim on me."

"You can be coldhearted."

Fargo met her stare. "You're like a lot of women. They let a man kiss them and think from then on all they have to do is snap their fingers, and the man will do whatever they ask."

"That's not what I think at all. But if you did with that Indian girl what you were about to do with me, I would be the world's worst fool to let you do it now, wouldn't I?"

"Only if you were expecting me to propose, after."

"Coldhearted," Angeline repeated, and angrily strode to her tent. The flap closed with a snap.

Sighing, Fargo raised his cup.

"Woman trouble on top of everything else? You must not be living right, pard." McKern hunkered across the fire, his Sharps across his legs.

"What do you want?"

McKern held both hands out. "Hey, now. Don't bite my head off. I don't care who you poke." McKern grinned. "Although I will admit I'm plumb amazed at how females fall over themselves to get your britches off. What's your secret?"

"Regular baths."

"Hell, if that's all it takes, I'll go from one bath a year to maybe one a month."

"Did you come over here just to talk females?"

"No. But now that I know you're so popular with the contrary sex, I welcome any secrets you care to share."

"At your age? You old goat."

"Old ain't dead. I admire a pretty gal as much as the next gent. So tell me." McKern paused. "When are you fixing to poke Edith Havard?"

Fargo nearly snorted coffee up his nose. After he stopped laughing, he replied, "I wouldn't poke that old prune if we were the last people on earth. I'd bet that Theodore has to beg for it, if she even spreads her legs for him at all anymore."

"I could have done without that in my head, thank you very much." McKern gave a slight shake. "Now I'll have nightmares." He sobered. "But enough of this poking talk. Who do you think cut Strath free?"

"Whoever sent him after me the first time."

"Which could be anyone."

"Allen Havard is at the top of the list, but without proof I can't pistol-whip him." As much as Fargo would like to.

"Mrs. Havard's not too fond of you, either. Which amazes me, her being female."

"Keep it up."

"Anytime you need your back watched, give a holler."

"I'm obliged."

"Well, I just wanted to let you know I'm always ready to back your play." McKern smiled and walked off.

Presently, Fargo turned in. He slept fitfully, his Colt in his hand, waking whenever a sentry came anywhere near his blankets. A pink blush banded the eastern horizon when he threw his blankets off and sat up. Since he couldn't sleep, he might as well get up.

He wasn't the only early riser.

Cosmo was mixing flour and water in a bowl. "Good morning, Mr. Fargo. Quite the commotion last night, wasn't there?"

"Is that what you call it when one man tries to kill another? I thought the word for that is 'murder.'"

"Your sarcasm is duly noted. But I assure you I was as appalled as everyone else. To think that Mr. Strath would take it into his head to so something like that. It makes no sense."

"It does when you know he was paid. A lot of money, too."

"He told you that?"

Fargo nodded.

"My word. Wait. A lot of money? Surely you don't think one of the Havards is to blame?"

"No one else here has more money than they know what to do with," Fargo mentioned.

"Granted. But to what end? I'd imagine you suspect Allen. But that petty disagreement you had is hardly cause to have you killed."

"He might not think so."

Fargo skipped breakfast. He saddled the Ovaro and rode in a wide circle around the camp, scouring the ground for sign. He found nothing helpful.

The Havards were up and eating when he returned. Angeline wouldn't look at him. He told Theodore to keep heading north. "I'm going on ahead to scout."

"I suggest you be careful. You would be difficult to replace at this point, and I'd rather not have to go through the inconvenience."

"We wouldn't want that."

Teit was helping her grandfather to his feet. Her smile was warm and genuine. "It is a good morning to be alive," she said, and breathed deep of the crisp air.

"Let's hope we all stay that way." Fargo went to lift the reins but she put her hand on his leg.

"Wait. Before you go, I must warn you. It is not safe."

"What was your first clue?"

"Sorry? I am talking about my people. Ever since the war with the whites there has been—what is the expression?—bad blood. Many Nlaka'pamux resent the whites for coming to our land. There is much hate. A few of our young warriors want to drive the whites out, but our leaders counsel against spilling blood."

"Let me guess. The young ones spill white blood anyway."

"There is talk, yes. Every moon or so certain young warriors leave our village. They are gone for many sleeps. After they come back, we hear talk of whites who have disappeared."

Fargo touched her shoulder. "Thanks for the warning. I'll

keep my eyes skinned." He uncurled and was set to tap his spurs when she gripped the stirrup.

"There is more."

Fargo waited.

"One of those young warriors is my brother. My heart would be sad if anything happened to him."

Fargo almost said, "Then he shouldn't go around killing people." Instead he responded, "The odds of me running into them are pretty slim."

"Perhaps not," Teit said. "They watch the trails and this is one the whites use a lot."

Now Fargo had more to worry about. He rode alertly down to the valley floor. There, he paralleled the grassy bank of a swift stream to a sawtooth ridge. A game trail brought him to the crest. Below lay Fraser Canyon. He had come out north of the canyon mouth and the settlement of Yale.

Fraser Canyon was a turbulent tear in mother earth. In parts it was over three thousand feet deep. Sheer cliffs overlooked some of its serpentine length. Elsewhere, steep slopes, many with timber, many without. The narrow trail, which Fargo could see from the rim, was treacherous. A single misstep, and a person plunged to his doom. Word had it that more than a dozen people had done just that.

Fargo dismounted. He wrapped the reins around a tree limb. Moving to the edge, he spotted several men leading pack mules up the canyon toward the next settlement. As best he could recollect, the next one was called Spuzzum. Sixteen miles past Spuzzum was the Havards' destination, the last place Kenneth had been: Boston Bar.

Fargo pushed his hat back on his head. He would be glad when this was over. A full poke and a week or two in San Francisco promised a time he wouldn't soon forget.

The prospectors, if that was what they were, never looked up. One of the mules was being contrary and the man leading it had to keep pulling to get it to move.

A short way ahead of them was a stand of pines.

Fargo was watching the antics of the mule and not the stand, so he almost missed the movement. Someone was in the trees. Several someones, in fact. More prospectors, he figured, and didn't give it any more thought until one made the mistake of stepping into an open space between trees. The black hair and the buckskins told Fargo that those in the trees were Indians.

The white men with the mules were getting closer.

Now the warriors were spreading out, both above and below the trail. It was an ambush.

Fargo cupped his hands to his mouth. "Look out!" he shouted at the top of his lungs. His voice bounced off the cliff opposite, and echoed. "There are hostiles in the pines!"

The prospectors looked up but kept on walking as if everything were perfectly fine.

Fargo figured the echo had made it hard for them to understand. He tried again, bellowing, "Indians! Ahead of you!"

One of the men shielded his eyes with a hand.

"Hostiles!" Fargo tried yet again, waving his arms. He motioned at the pines.

The men kept going.

Fargo wondered if maybe they couldn't hear him because of the rapids below. Several of the warriors in the trees had glanced up and were talking among themselves.

Whirling, Fargo dashed to the Ovaro and yanked the Henry from the saddle scabbard. He levered a round into the chamber, ran back to the edge, and wedged the stock to his shoulder.

By now the prospectors and the mules were less than fifty feet from the pines.

Fargo couldn't see any of the warriors. But they were there, waiting for their unsuspecting victims to get within arrow range.

Fargo aimed at a point on the narrow trail about ten feet in front of the first prospector. He stroked the trigger and the Henry kicked. Down below, a geyser of dirt testified to his accuracy. He lowered the rifle.

The men had stopped and were looking up.

Fargo jumped up and down and waved his arms again. "Indians in the trees ahead! Watch yourselves!"

The last man in line raised a rifle and fired.

The *spang* of lead striking rock caused Fargo to jump back. The lunkheads were shooting at him! Fargo poked his head over the rim and tried once more. "Hostiles! Don't go any farther!"

Another shot whizzed past.

"Damn idiots." Fargo was at a loss. If they kept on, they would be slaughtered. But how could he stop them when they were shooting at him? He risked another look.

The three men were twenty feet from the stand and looking up at the rim, not at the trees.

"Indians, damn you!"

The lead man brought his mule to a stop and the others did the same. They talked back and forth, and gestured. The second man pointed at the river and then up at Fargo and put a hand to his ear.

"Hostiles in the trees!"

All three were looking up but they didn't raise their rifles. Fargo showed himself and jabbed an arm at the pines. The last man said something, and the man in the middle raised an arm and waved.

"Hell," Fargo said.

They moved toward the stand.

Fargo started to curse.

The first prospector and his mule entered the pines. Then the second, and the third. Fargo couldn't see any of them. He listened for war whoops and shots but the canyon was quiet, save for the river and the wind.

Fargo dropped into a crouch. "Where the hell are you?"

A mule came out of the other side of the stand. Then the second animal. But not the third. Both were trotting.

Then a prospector staggered out, his hands over his belly. Ropy coils of intestines were spilling out. The prospector weaved. He cried off. He looked up at Fargo, and stepped off the trail into space. He screamed all the way down.

Fargo swore some more. Something brushed the back of his head. A fly, he thought, and swatted at it.

But it wasn't a fly.

It was a gun barrel.

11

If the Knife warrior had simply snuck up on him, put the muzzle of the rifle to the back of Fargo's head, and pulled the trigger without saying anything, Fargo would have died then and there. But Fargo was in luck; the warrior wanted to take him alive. Instead of shooting, he commanded, "Not move, white dog."

But even as the warrior spoke, Fargo sidestepped and whirled. He moved so fast that although the warrior instantly fired, the slug tore through empty space instead of Fargo's head.

Fargo dropped the Henry but only so he could grab the barrel of the warrior's rifle and wrench it from the surprised man's grasp.

The Knife sprang back and resorted to his blade.

Reversing his grip, Fargo swung the rifle like a club. It was an old single-shot flintlock, heavy and long. The warrior ducked, or tried to; the stock clipped him across the temple. Stunned, he staggered back, gave his head a few hard shakes, and recovered.

A vicious snarl twisted his features.

"I'm not your enemy," Fargo said, doubting it would do any good. He was right.

The Knife hissed and attacked, coming in swift and low, his blade spearing at Fargo's groin. Fargo swung at the man's wrist to knock the knife from his hand, but the warrior sprang to one side and circled.

Fargo did some swift thinking. The warrior must be with those below. Maybe he was their lookout. Or maybe they had horses hidden for a getaway and this one was watching the horses.

Fargo did the unexpected. He threw the rifle at him. The man skipped aside and the rifle missed, as Fargo knew it would. But throwing it bought him the split second he needed to draw his Colt and thumb back the hammer. He almost fired. But then he remembered Teit saying that one of the *young warriors was her brother, and how sad she would be if anything happened to him.* The odds were slim that this was the one. But Fargo had learned the hard way that life had a habit of springing unwanted surprises. "Are you Teit's brother?"

The young warrior had turned to stone when the Colt materialized in Fargo's hand. He glanced from the six-shooter to Fargo's face and his dark eyes glittered hate. But he didn't attack. "You know Teit?"

"I met her and her grandfather, Chelahit. They're coming back from visiting his brother."

Uncertainty replaced some of the hate. "I not her brother." He began to back toward the trees.

"I can't let you leave," Fargo said. "Your friends killed white men down in the canyon."

"We kill all whites!" the warrior boasted. "This land ours. We not want whites here. Leave!"

Fargo extended his arm. "Not another step."

With supreme contempt, the warrior turned. "You want kill, shoot me in back." And with that, he jogged into the woods.

Against his better judgment Fargo let him go. He had a feeling he would regret it. Unhappy with himself, he let down the hammer and twirled the Colt into his holster.

Fargo remembered the men down below and ran to the edge. There was no sign of anyone. The two mules were hurrying up the trail. There was no sign of the third or their human masters.

"Damn it."

Fargo picked up the Henry, brushed dust from the receiver, and hiked a short way long the rim in both directions. It was as if the earth had opened up and swallowed the Nlaka'pamux.

That was all he could do for now. Fargo forked leather and headed back.

The others were just entering the last valley.

McKern was riding point and greeted him with a wave and a smile. But the smile faded when Fargo drew rein. "Say there, hoss. You look as if you were stung by a scorpion."

"Any trouble while I was away?"

"Not a lick, if you don't count Theodore and Edith squabbling over something or other, and Allen saying as how all these evergreens are bad for his complexion."

"He said what?"

"Those are his exact words. I heard him with my own ears." McKern gazed at the thick forests that thronged the high slopes. "Beats the hell out of me what he's talking about. Folks don't go around rubbing trees on their faces."

Fargo gazed the length of the long line. "Keep them going. I want to reach the canyon by nightfall."

"We're close, I take it."

"So is a Knife war party." Fargo gigged the Ovaro and soon came to Theodore and Cosmo.

Reining the Ovaro around so he could pace them, Fargo related what he had seen in the canyon.

"Those stinking savages!" was Theodore's reaction. "The world would be a better place if every Indian was wiped out."

"Some of them say the same about white men."

"Yes, and how ironic is that? The inferior wanting to wipe out the superior."

"You are one bigoted son of a bitch."

Theodore went rigid with resentment. "Here now. With what I'm paying you, I deserve a little respect."

"Damn little."

Cosmo said, "Don't take it personal, Theodore. Mr. Fargo has lived with Indians, as I recall. He regards them differently than we do."

"You, too?" Fargo said.

"I don't hate them on general principle, if that's what you're asking. But they *are* savages. They live in dwellings made of animal hides and wear animal skins for clothes."

Fargo looked down at his buckskins.

"Before the white man came along they spent all their time making war on one another. They are at best a nuisance and at worst a menace, and either way, yes, I agree with Theodore. We are better off without them. The common saying that the only good Indian is a dead Indian is exactly right."

"And you so cultured and all."

Cosmo showed a rare trace of irritation. "What are you implying? Can you speak three languages? Can you cook a soufflé? Can you discourse on the theater and fashion and politics? I take great pride in being cultured, thank you very much."

"All that, and modest, too."

"Now you are merely being a bore. If you have nothing more enlightening to say, go be a bore elsewhere."

"Don't mind if I do." Fargo rode to where Edith was glumly regarding the world and brought the Ovaro next to her. "How are you holding up, Mrs. Havard?"

"What do you care?"

"I'm only being polite," Fargo lied. It was about time he had his hunch about Theodore confirmed. "I tried talking to your husband and Cosmo but they didn't want my company."

Edith's glower deepened. "Look at them. Together, as always. My husband and that *thing*."

"Is that what you call your butler?"

Edith glanced sharply at him and shook so violently, she

appeared to on the verge of throwing a fit. "Butler, hell. Are you blind? He's an abomination."

"I take it you don't like Cosmo."

"I *hate* him. I rue the day he came into our lives. Him and his constant fawning over Theodore. He doesn't fool me. He doesn't fool me one bit."

"He doesn't?" Fargo prompted when she didn't go on.

"Cosmo is after Theo's money. He hopes to be in Theo's will and receive a large inheritance. So he babies my Theo. And Theo, the idiot, treats Cosmo as if Cosmo walks on air!"

"You don't say."

"I saw right through Cosmo from the start. His oily smiles and little gestures. He disgusts me. Why, there are times when he acts more like a woman than I do. Can you imagine?"

"It's a strange world," Fargo said.

"Mine was an orderly world before he came along. My world was proper. Theodore and I weren't always the most compatible of couples but we had a good marriage. Then this man came along and drove a wedge between us. I wish Cosmo were dead."

"I had no idea," Fargo said with a straight face.

"That's because you're not female. Women have a sense about these things. We're not as easily duped."

"I'll be sure to remember that." Fargo touched his hat brim and moved down the line to the next pair.

Angeline and Allen were talking but stopped when he brought the Ovaro around.

"What do you want?" Allen immediately snapped.

"To warn you there is a war party hereabouts."

Angeline held her chin higher. "Maybe you can ask your Indian friend if she will talk to them about leaving us be."

Allen snickered. "That's a good one, sis."

"I have it figured out," Fargo said.

They looked at each other, and Angeline asked, "Have what figured out, pray tell?"

"Why Kenneth left home." With that parting shot, Fargo went on past the rest until he came to Teit and Chelahit. She smiled up at him.

"I am glad you made it back."

"I almost didn't." Again Fargo told about the war party, only in more detail.

Both became troubled. Chelahit bowed his head as if in great shame.

"I am sorry for what they have done," Teit said sincerely. "Unless they are stopped there will be another war."

"They're your people. Why don't the Nlaka'pamux stop them?"

"A Knife never harms another Knife, and that is what it would take. Their hate is too strong. They will not stop killing until they are under the ground."

"That won't be long if they keep it up."

Teit sighed. "It is too bad people cannot get along. Think of how wonderful life would be."

"I'm not one for fairy tales."

The last rider was, as usual, Rohan, leading the pack animals. He grinned as Fargo came up.

"You and your hair are still together."

"I had to work at it." For the last time Fargo explained about the war party. He left out the part about letting the one warrior live.

"They don't worry me none." Rohan patted his shotgun. "So long as they let me be, I'll let them be." He ran a sleeve across his mouth. "I'm more interested in reaching Yale so I can wet my throat."

"I like my liquor, too," Fargo admitted.

"There are days when I like it too much. I wake up under a table, wondering how in hell I got there. Or the time I came around in a stable loft, as naked as the day I was born." Rohan laughed. "You should have seen the looks I got when I walked out of that stable with a handful of straw over my private parts."

"How are the packhorses holding up?"

"Fine. Just fine. I take good care of them. Horses don't lie and cheat and leave you for another man who isn't half the man you are."

"You had a wife once?"

"If you can call her that. She drank worse than I do and had a roving eye. The only reason I ever said 'I do' is that I was too drunk to know who I was 'I doing.'"

That evening they camped on the canyon rim. Fires were started and everyone settled down. There were enough of them that an attack seemed unlikely but Fargo added an extra sentry anyway. He was sipping coffee when McKern hastened out of the dark.

"I thought you should know. They're gone."

Fargo didn't ask who.

"They slipped away while we were setting up camp. I was busy or I'd have noticed sooner."

"I expected it," Fargo said.

"Here's something you didn't expect. Theodore Havard has given orders that from here on out, we're to shoot any and all Knife Indians we see on sight. Allen spread the word."

"Like hell we will."

The patriarch and his cultured shadow were by the tents. Fargo dispensed with the niceties and waded right into them.

"What the hell do you think you're doing?"

Theodore was watching Cosmo polish his shoes. "I gather that you are referring to my edict about the Indians?"

"Many of the Nlaka'pamux are friendly. Start shooting every one you see and you'll kill some who never harmed a white. You'll also bring the whole tribe down on our heads."

"Better safe than sorry," Theodore said without looking up from his shoes.

Fargo grabbed his arm. "Listen to me, damn you. The British won't like it, either."

Cosmo said, "Let go of Theodore."

"They'll throw you out of British Columbia and you'll never find your son."

"Didn't you hear me?" Cosmo stood. "I told you to let go of him."

"He's hurting my arm," Theodore said.

Cosmo hit Fargo.

12

Fargo wasn't expecting it. He didn't regard Cosmo as the kind to take swings at people. The punch almost caught him on the jaw, but he had caught the movement out of the corner of his eye and started to jerk his head aside. The blow only grazed him. Even so, he was knocked back a step.

"I told you to let go of Theodore."

Fargo ignored the pain and shook his head to clear it. He heard Theodore laugh and Allen titter and saw Cosmo's smug smile, and from deep inside of him exploded pure, potent rage. He tore into Cosmo with his fists flying and sent the butler sprawling onto his back.

Silence fell.

Cosmo looked more surprised than hurt. He rubbed his jaw and said quietly, "You shouldn't have done that."

"Are you all right?" Theodore asked, bending to help him up.

"Stand back," Cosmo said. He stood and raised his fists in a boxing stance. "Unfortunately for you, Mr. Fargo, I can't let that pass. I am going to thrash you within an inch of your life."

"Cosmo, don't," Theodore urged.

Edith said, "Let him if he wants. It's about time someone put him in his place, and I suspect our guide is just the man to do it."

That brought a smile from Cosmo. "I would expect that from you, Mrs. Havard."

"You think you know me but you don't," was her retort.

Fargo barely listened. He was growing sick and tired of the whole bunch. They thought they were better than everyone else. They hated everyone with different skin. They looked down their noses at the world. Mired in the quicksand of their hate, they were a blight on life.

"You have one out," Cosmo said. "Apologize to Theodore and I might not punish you."

Allen threw in, "Don't hold back on my father's account. Show our simple excuse for a frontiersman that he's not so high and mighty."

Fargo spun and caught Allen with a solid right. Allen went down, and Fargo whirled just as Cosmo closed on him. Fargo was mildly surprised that the man wasn't all brag. Cosmo could fight. He threw hard punches, and blocked and countered smoothly.

Fargo was no slouch himself. He had been in a hundred fights and brawls, and he called on that experience to chip away at Cosmo like a master sculptor at a block of marble. More and more of his blows got through.

Cosmo grew red in the face. He unleashed jabs, crosses, and uppercuts.

Fargo blocked, sidestepped, slipped. Then he planted himself and wouldn't be moved. A blow jarred his forearm. Knuckles glanced off his cheek. He waited for the opening that was bound to come, for the mistake Cosmo was bound to make.

Head-to-head they slugged away.

Cosmo was more on the defensive now.

Fargo uncorked a left and the butler sidestepped. He blocked a looping right. It left Cosmo open for a moment, and a moment was all Fargo needed. His fist connected solidly and Cosmo staggered. Fargo followed through with an uppercut that ended with his fist high in the air and Cosmo lying on the ground.

"Cosmo!" Theodore cried.

Fargo stood over him. "You ever lay a hand on me again—"
He didn't finish his warning.

Cosmo did a strange thing. He smiled, then moved his jaw
back and forth. "Nothing is broken, Theodore. But I'll be sore
in the morning." He looked at Fargo. "Well? Are you just going to stand there?"

"Let him up, you brute," Theodore said.

Fargo turned. "There will be no killing Indians unless we're
attacked. Savvy?"

"You overstep yourself," Theodore said indignantly. "But I
suppose if I don't agree, you'll report me to the British."

"No, I'll shoot you."

Theodore blinked. "I honestly think you would. But I don't
like being threatened. I don't like it at all."

"Do as he wants, Theodore," Cosmo said. "Finding Kenneth is more important than our pride."

"I should fire him."

Fargo would gladly be shed of them, but he had given his
word and he would get them to Boston Bar. "That's your
choice, mister."

Theodore glanced at Cosmo, who shook his head. "Very
well. I'll overlook your outrageous conduct this time. But
from here on out I don't want you anywhere near Cosmo or
my family unless it is required in the performance of your
duties. Is that clear?"

"Don't prod me." Fargo turned to walk off and discovered
McKern holding his Sharps on Allen, who had a hand under
his jacket.

"I caught this one fixing to shoot you."

Fargo brushed Allen's jacket aside, and sure enough, Allen
had his hand on a derringer in a small holster on his belt.
Fargo snatched it out and jiggled it on his palm.

"Here now. That's mine."

"You'll get it back when I'm good and ready."

"Father! Do something."

Disgust flooding through him, Fargo walked off. McKern came along, stepping sideways with his Sharps pointed at the Havards.

"I wouldn't put it past them to gun you in the back, hoss."

Fargo didn't say anything.

"They are just about the most useless family there ever was. If it was me, I'd tell them what I think of them and go my own way."

"I might yet," Fargo said.

They had gone far enough that McKern lowered his Sharps, then chuckled.

"It warmed my heart to see you pound on that uppity servant or whatever he is."

"Another enemy to add to the list."

"Don't you worry none. I've offered to watch your back, remember? I hope they give me cause to blow them to hell. Any one of them."

Everyone else had witnessed the fight and was standing around uncertain of what to do. Fargo solved that by bellowing, "We head for Yale at first light. I'd get plenty of rest were I you."

Rohan was by the other fire, drinking coffee. "I'd have paid good money to see you put fancy pants in his place like you did. Any chance I can talk you into doing the same to Edith? She is always on me about that mare of hers. How I better treat it special or else." He chuckled. "It's women like her that make some gents swear off females."

McKern said, "I wouldn't mind getting hitched one day. Provided I can find me a gal who won't talk my head off or nag me to tears or try to change me into someone I'm not."

"Then you'll never be hitched," Rohan said. "There's no such critter."

Fargo squatted and filled a cup and took deep breaths to help his rage subside.

"What I want to know," McKern said, "is whether the stories I've heard about Yale are true. They say it's wild and woolly, and no place for amateurs."

"It was in the gold rush days," Rohan said.

"In that case I look forward to a bottle of their best. I've been without bug juice for too long."

"You and me both."

Fargo could use a stiff drink, himself. Several stiff drinks, in fact.

Later that night, as he lay under his blankets with his head on his saddle, Fargo was awakened by a nicker from the Ovaro. He rolled over and slid his hand to his Colt. The camp was still. A fire crackled and the sentries were awake and alert. He probed the shadows but saw nothing. After a while his eyelids grew leaden and he drifted off again.

By noon the next day they reached Yale. Built on the bank of the Fraser River just south of the mouth of Fraser Canyon, it had a reputation for being Sodom and Gomorrah rolled into one. At the height of the gold rush more than fifteen thousand souls had indulged in every vice known and then some. Since then the population had dwindled to between seven and eight thousand, but it was still as carnal as ever.

Fargo enjoyed the bustle and hubbub. Even though it was the middle of the day, the saloons were open and busy. Tinny music, the babble of voices, laughter—all testified to fine times being had. Painted ladies sashayed about, displaying their wares and getting a dash of sun. Down at the river the landings were lined with dozens of riverboats, large and small, including half a dozen steamers.

The grandest hotel was called the Fraser. Fargo drew rein near the hitch rail but didn't dismount.

The Havards were riding together for once, with Cosmo slightly behind them. Theodore came over near Fargo and halted. Taking a handkerchief from his pocket, he mopped at his face and coughed.

"All this dust is a nuisance. And look at the horse and dog droppings everywhere. Don't these people care?"

"It's despicable," Edith carped. "Living in filth and sin. I wouldn't be caught dead here if it weren't for Kenneth."

Allen wore the sly grin of a fox loose in a chicken coop. "I don't know, Mother. It appeals to me."

"It would," Angeline said.

Fargo jerked a thumb at the hotel. "I figured this is where you would want to stay. We'll rest up, buy what supplies we need, and head up the canyon in the morning."

"Why waste half a day?" Edith asked. "I'm not that tired."

"I'm not thinking of you. I'm thinking of the horses. They can do with some grain."

Theodore leaned on his saddle horn and coughed some more. "Who do you think you're fooling, Mr. Fargo? I heard some of the men talking. The real reason they want to stay the night is so they can drink and gamble and womanize."

"Can you blame them after weeks on the trail?"

"I can," Edith said. "Wallowing in this muck like so many pigs. Where's their dignity?"

"In a bottle of whiskey or a woman's arms. Or maybe both."

"Honestly, I never."

"Three times at least," Fargo said.

They were slow to catch on. Then Edith colored and Allen laughed and Angeline looked fit to punch Fargo.

"Are you going to let this creature talk to me like that?" Edith demanded of her husband.

"I can't very well fault a man for telling the truth, now can I, my dear?" Theodore responded.

On that note Fargo left them to check in while he sought a stable. It was full but the corral out back had plenty of space. Oats could be had for three times what oats would cost south of the border. Fortunately Theodore was paying expenses.

The men gathered out front. They were like a pack of bloodhounds eager to be off on a scent.

Rohan licked his lips in anticipation. "The first thing I aim to do is find me a female."

McKern chuckled. "Maybe the first thing you should do is take a hot bath."

"Why waste the money? It's not March."

"What does March have to do with soap and water?"

"I treat myself to a bath once a year on the day I was born, March seventh. Whether I need it or not."

"You need it."

Fargo decided to get a word in. "We meet here tomorrow at sunrise. Any man who shows up late loses half their pay."

"Half?" a man repeated. "That's harsh."

"Hell," said another. "I'm liable to be so hungover, my head will fall off."

"Carry it with you," Fargo replied. "Sunrise and no later. We still have a ways to go to reach Boston Bar, and I want an early start. Now scat."

A bevy of quail could not have scattered faster. All except one. McKern cradled his Sharps and said, "I thought I'd tag along with you, sonny, if that's all right. I never did like to drink alone."

Fargo didn't mind. In fact, something had been preying on him, and as they walked along reading the names of the saloons, he gave voice to a question. "It was you who shot Strath the other night, wasn't it?"

McKern broke stride. "What makes you say that?"

"No two rifles sound alike. I used a Sharps for years, and I can tell a Sharps from any other kind. The shot that killed Strath came from a Sharps, and only one other man besides you has one."

"Damn."

"Mind explaining?"

McKern shrugged. "He was a weasel. He'd tried to kill you once. So when I spotted him sneaking from camp, I went after him. I lost him in the woods, but then I heard you and him fighting. I was surprised when you didn't kill him."

"So you shot him?"

"Sooner or later he'd have tried to kill you again. And I've taken a shine to you, hoss."

"Hell."

"When I heard him say he wouldn't tell you who put him up to it, I snuck off a ways and shot the bastard. Then I ran up with the others and acted all innocent." McKern paused. "You're not going to hold it against me, are you?"

"Edith Havard would."

"That she-goat would turn me over to the Brits."

"I have something else in mind."

"Such as?"

"Such as treating you to a drink." Fargo grinned and clapped McKern on the back. As he did, he happened to glance back.

Allen Havard was following them.

13

"What do you reckon the peckerwood is up to?"

Fargo and McKern were in a saloon called the Lucky Strike. They had bellied up to the bar and the bartender had brought them whiskeys. Fargo shrugged and downed his at a gulp, then said to the barkeep, "Leave the bottle." He paid and led McKern to one of the few empty tables. He sat facing the entrance.

"Say the word and I'll go over there and beat on him some." McKern patted the stock of his Sharps. "I can do it so that what few brains he has will leak out."

"We don't know for sure he's up to no good."

"Even if he's not, I'm tired of his shenanigans. You must be, too." McKern sipped and shifted his chair. "Look at him over yonder, hiding behind those ore hounds, thinking we haven't caught on."

"He's a city boy."

"So that makes him naturally stupid? If you ask me, you've put up with more than you should. If you won't let me bust him over the head, how about if we get him to follow us and we jump him so you can ask what in hell he's up to?"

"If it comes to that, we will," Fargo said. "But for now we'll wait for him to show his hand. And speaking of hands . . ." Fargo had noticed a poker game with a chair open.

"You're a puzzlement, son. You truly are."

"The more rope we give him, the more likely he is to hang himself."

"I take it back. You're not a puzzlement. You're one of the most devious sons of bitches I've ever met." McKern laughed.

"Care to watch me win some money?"

Fargo moved to the poker table. He inserted himself into the game, placed his poke on the table, and his very first hand was a full house. A promising start, he thought. But his cards ran more cold than hot, and after an hour he was barely five dollars to the better.

McKern hovered at his back, watching and occasionally asking questions of the other players: What was the latest news hereabouts? Any big strikes lately? Had the Knifes been acting up?

That last question interested Fargo. One of the players remarked that the Knifes never stopped acting up, that the Fraser Canyon War hadn't settled anything.

Another man commented, "Whites disappear all the time but the sheriff can't seem to find those to blame. A lot of us think he's not trying very hard."

"Why not?" McKern responded.

"The British tread lightly where the Knifes are concerned. They don't want another uprising on their hands."

"Wipe the red devils out," yet another player said. "That's what I'd do.

It's the only way to put an end to it."

Fargo interjected, "I've heard there's a lot of bad blood between the whites and the Nlaka'pamux."

"Hell, mister, you don't know the half of it. There's nothing but hate on both sides."

"This whole territory is a powder keg waiting to explode," was another's opinion. "Mark my words. Before this year is out, there will be a second war that will make the first seem like a church social."

Fargo's cards went completely cold and he quit the game with winnings of two dollars. The bottle was about empty, so he drained it and paid for another. McKern at his side, he walked out and stood under the overhang, watching the flow of humanity on the busy street.

"Where did that weak sister get to? I haven't seen him in a while."

"You'll give yourself a crick in your neck if you're not careful," Fargo advised.

"He's an itch you won't let me scratch and I can't stand itches," McKern grumbled.

They strolled along, taking in the sights. Gilded doves smiled and winked. A redhead wearing a green dress that left little to the imagination came up to them and glanced from Fargo to McKern and back again, then slowly ran a fingertip from her flat belly to the junction of her swelling breasts.

"How would you two gents like the time of your life?"

McKern grinned and asked, "Who goes first?"

"I was thinking both of you at the same time," she said in a husky whisper, and curled her red lips. "I make twice the money twice as fast."

"At the same time?" McKern actually blushed. "Damn, girl. Do it in the middle of the street, why don't you? Me, I like to poke by my lonesome."

"Just you and nobody else?" The gilded minx laughed.

"You young tart, I should take you over my knee and spank you."

"Please do. I love to be spanked as much as I love anything." She turned to Fargo and lightly touched his chin. "How about you, handsome? Are you as shy as gramps here?"

"Shyness is one trait no one has ever accused me of."

McKern had swelled up like a riled rooster. "Who in hell are you calling 'gramps,' girl? I'll have you know I'm a long ways from seventy and as spry as men half my age."

"Come up to my room and show me how spry," the redhead offered. "Your handsome friend can wait his turn out in the hall if that's how you want it to be."

"Maybe later," Fargo said. "Where would we find you?"

The redhead gave directions. "Now be sure to come, you hear? If I'm not there, wait around. If I'm with another gentleman, I tie a ribbon to the latch. Otherwise, just knock." She giggled and patted McKern's cheek and swayed off.

"Damn," McKern said. "What is this world coming to? The women get more brazen every year."

"I admire her spunk."

"Spunk, nothing. Did you smell her perfume? And that body of hers! I could use a dunk in the river right about now." He cocked his head. "You going to take her up on it?"

"We'll see."

A commotion drew them to a fistfight. Two prospectors were going at one another, hand and foot and tooth, punching and kicking and biting while rolling around in the dirt and the droppings. Both were drunk and, for all their flailing, doing little damage. A small crowed had gathered and was laughing and yelling for the combatants to fight harder.

Then one of the men bit down on the other's ear, and blood spurted. That brought yips of glee from onlookers.

"That's the spirit!"

"Rip his ear off!"

"Or his nose!"

McKern nudged Fargo. "The folks in these parts ain't much for the milk of human kindness."

"It's not just these parts," Fargo said.

They came to the end of the long street. To the north Fraser Canyon reared, the river winding along in its depths, the high walls shadowy and forbidding in the fading light of the setting sun.

"Spooky-looking," McKern said.

"You've seen canyons before."

"Folks say this is one of the worst. The trail in has killed more men than smallpox."

"A few," Fargo allowed, and glanced at the oldster. "What kills most of them is bad nerves."

"I get what you're saying. And if my nerves need soothing, there's always our lady friend."

Just then several Indians came out of the canyon, heading into Yale. The three were talking and smiling and one bobbed his head as they went by.

"They seemed friendly enough," McKern commented.

"It only takes a few bad apples."

Fargo turned to retrace their steps.

The three Indians had come up on four white men coming the other way. Neither group moved aside for the other. They all stopped, and one of the white men said something and patted a revolver he wore butt forward on his right hip. The Indians looked at one another and went around the four whites, who sneered and laughed.

"Yes, sir," McKern said drily, "I doubt there's a drop of milk anywhere in Yale."

The quartet kept on coming. They stopped a few yards off, blocking the way, their thumbs hooked in belts, their chins outthrust, their hard eyes defiant.

Fargo pegged them as swaggering toughs. All wore six-shooters, a mix of models, Remington and Smith & Wesson and Bisley and a Colt. The men were unkempt, their clothes dirty, but no more so than most of Yale's inhabitants. The second man on the right, the one who had said something to the Indians, had a constant pinched look, as if he had just sucked on a lemon. His voice was high and reedy.

"What do we have here, boys? An old geezer and a plainsman."

McKern regarded them with annoyance. "What the hell do you idiots want?"

"Watch who you're calling names, old man."

"Watch who you're calling 'old,' you damn pup," McKern shot back. "I don't carry this rifle for bluff or ballast."

The cruel-faced one uttered a brittle chuckle. "Will you listen to this old fart? Threatening *us*."

One of the others said, "We need to learn him some manners, Santee."

Yet another added, "They say you can't teach an old dog new tricks. Let's see if that's true."

McKern was red in the face again and growing redder. "I'd like to see you try. Any of you. I'll damn well bed you down permanent."

"We're real scared, old man," Santee said.

Fargo finally spoke, quiet and low. "You should be."

The four focused on him. Santee looked him up and down and said, "What do we have to be scared about?"

"Dying."

A wariness came over them, a tenseness in their postures and in their expressions. Santee showed it the least, but the hand hooked in his belt moved a fraction nearer his six-gun.

"Well, now, I do believe this gent is telling us to back off or he'll blow out our wicks."

"How much did he pay you?" Fargo asked.

All four visibly stiffened.

"What are you babbling about?" Santee demanded.

"Allen Havard. How much did he pay you? And what is it he paid you to do? Try to scare us? Cripple us? Kill us, maybe?"

"Mister, I don't know what in hell you're talking about. I never heard of any Havard."

Fargo took a step to one side, his right hand brushing his holster. "Whatever he paid you, it wasn't enough."

"Now you just hold on," a straw-haired man said. "There was no talk of swapping lead."

"Shut up, Mitch," Santee said.

Mitch did no such thing. "I don't like the looks of this hombre. If it's a pistol fight, you can count me out."

Santee's eyes glittered with anger. "I always knew you were a no-account, Mitch."

The man named Mitch backed away, his hands palms out.

"Don't even think it. Not in broad daylight. Not with the street packed with people. There will be too many witnesses."

"I'll gut you for this."

Mitch continued to back away until he bumped into someone. Turning, he clomped hastily off, fearfully glancing over his shoulder.

Fargo said, "And then it was three to one."

"Three to two," McKern amended.

"Stay out of this."

"Like hell. We're pards, ain't we?"

"It's me they were paid to jump."

Santee was practically boiling with fury. "I haven't said that. I haven't said anything."

"You don't have to." Fargo took another step and the three shifted so they faced him. Now they had their backs to the front wall of an assay office. If one of Fargo's slugs went all the way through, there was less chance of hitting a bystander.

The other two men looked at Santee. It was plain they didn't like the situation but were reluctant to say so.

McKern said, "Mind telling me how you knew Allen Havard put them up to it?"

"Why else was he shadowing us?" Fargo answered without taking his eyes off the curly wolves. "Strath failed so he hired this bunch."

Santee's hand moved a fraction. "You think you're so damn smart. I'll spit on your coffin, is what I'll do."

Fargo willed himself to relax. He took slow, easy breaths. His right hand began to tingle. "Whenever you're ready."

As whimsical fate would have it, an elderly matron wearing a blue dress and bonnet and using a cane chose that moment to walk by, passing between Fargo and the three toughs. She gave them a friendly smile.

"How do you do, ma'am?" McKern said.

The old woman paused and turned her wrinkled countenance to the sky. "I would do better if it wasn't for this awful heat. It's a wonder we don't all melt away."

Fargo watched Santee's hand, afraid the woman would be caught in a hail of lead. But Santee, to his surprise, had the decency to let her walk on. Or was it that shooting a female was bound to get him strung up?

"Now, then," Santee said, "I'm supposed to tell you that if you get on your horse and head back to the States, you can leave here alive."

"Make me," Fargo said.

14

Santee's smile was ice and insult. "I'm glad you want it this way. This will be a pleasure."

"Do you ever do more than talk?" Fargo braced for the explosion of violence to come.

Santee glanced at the other pair. "You heard him, boys. He can't get all three of us. Not if we draw at the same time. So when I count to three, we put holes in this son of a bitch." He paused, and the others poised to draw.

"How about if I do the counting?" Fargo said, and with lightning rapidity he barked, "One, two, three." Then his hand was down and out and they were stabbing for their hardware but they were much too slow. He shot Santee through the forehead, and for a fleeting instant, astonishment registered. He shot the other two—shot them so fast that they died on their feet, heartbeats apart. One pitched forward. The other oozed to the ground like so much slime.

McKern had started to raise his Sharps and now stood transfixed in disbelief. "God in heaven."

People on the street were scattering, thinking there might be more shots. Those who had seen the outcome and knew it was over gaped.

Fargo replaced the spent cartridges and twirled the Colt into his holster. "Let's go find the bastard who put them up to this."

"What about these?" McKern said, poking Santee's body.

"They can lie there and rot for all I care."

McKern took a step but abruptly stopped. "Hold on, hoss." Squatting, he went through their pockets and held out what he found. "Looks like one hundred dollars for each one. Not a lot for a killing."

"To them it probably was." Fargo got out of there before he was badgered with questions. Some of the onlookers were bound to want an explanation.

McKern divided the money and offered him half. "It's only fair."

They searched long and hard and high and low but saw no sign of Allen Havard. The other Havards were at a restaurant, along with Cosmo, who got up from the table and came over when Fargo motioned.

"We're just sitting down to eat. What can I do for you?"

"Where's Allen?"

"He went off by himself shortly after we arrived and I haven't seen him since. Why? Is something wrong?"

"I just wanted to talk to him." Fargo went out with a surprised McKern in tow.

"I don't savvy you, sonny. What didn't you tell him the truth?"

"That was the truth."

"You're not fixing to gun Allen the moment you set eyes on him? After what he did?"

"Santee never said he was the one."

"Did you expect he would? If it were me, I'd shoot the buzzard and be done with him. He doesn't deserve to go on breathing. Hell, I'll shoot him myself if you won't want to."

"And have the British authorities after you? No. This is between him and me."

McKern shook his head in confusion. "Damn if you make a lick of sense. But I'll do as you ask."

The Lucky Strike was their next stop. McKern bought another bottle. Fargo was more interested in the doves mingling with the customers. He settled on a saucy brunette who laughed a lot, and invited her to their table. She studied him over her glass and gave McKern a friendly wink.

"So now. My name is Maggie, and I'm pleased to meet you. Is it just drinks or will you be wanting more?"

"More for me," Fargo said.

"I'm glad to hear it. You're easy on a girl's eyes." Maggie grinned. "But there's no hurry on my account. I like to sit and talk just as much as I like the other."

"Talk about what?" McKern asked.

"Anything will do. Did you hear about the shooting earlier? Three men were gunned down out in the street. I knew one of them. Santee, he was called. If ever a man had it coming, it was him."

"You don't say."

"There are those who are the salt of the earth and there are those who are bastards. Santee wasn't salt." Maggie tilted her glass to her mouth. "Word is, a man was sent to fetch the sheriff, which is too bad. Whenever he's here, things quiet down. There's nothing like the law to put a damper on fine spirits."

"I like you, lady," McKern said.

So did Fargo. She had a pretty face with bright eyes and long eyelashes, and a bosom more ample than most. For half an hour they drank and talked, and at one point Maggie mentioned that several prospectors had disappeared and there was talk of reprisals against the Knife Indians, but she doubted anything would come of it. The British had made it clear to the Americans that anyone who incited another war would be thrown into prison and the key to their cell thrown into the river.

"It's gotten so, any white who says he thinks kindly of the Knife Indians is liable to be hauled into a dark alley and clubbed to death." Maggie put down her glass. "But I reckon I've sat here long enough. How about that room? And before I forget, I'm to ask for ten dollars in advance."

The room was small, the only furniture a bed. The door had a bolt and Fargo made sure to throw it. He hadn't seen any sign of Allen Havard. But it wasn't Allen he had to watch out for; it was the men Allen kept hiring to kill him. Which begged the question: Why? There had to be more to it than him calling Allen a jackass. A lot more.

Maggie was waiting with her hands on her hips. "Well? Are you just going to stand there?"

Fargo pulled her close and kissed her, hard. He was content to take his time but she wasn't. Her hand groped between his legs. She had a lot of experience, this one, and his pole was rigid iron in no time.

"Mmmmm," Maggie cooed when they broke for breath. "Nice. Very nice."

Fargo wasn't sure if she was talking about the kiss or lower down. He cupped both breasts and she ground her hips against him. Guiding her to the bed, he eased her onto her back. Almost immediately she pried at his buckle and his pants. His manhood sprang free.

"Oh my. You're a handful."

Doves knew not to wear dresses that took a man forever to get off. Lots of buttons and stays were for their more maidenly sisters. Maggie's had only three buttons and slid off her as easily as the bedspread off the bed. Lying there in her white undergarments with a leg crooked and a come-get-me look in her eyes, she was downright alluring.

"Like what you see, big man?"

Fargo let his actions speak for him. He sucked on a nipple. He rimmed her ear with the tip of his tongue and bit the lobe. He parted her thighs and knelt between her legs and gripped his redwood, about to enter her.

"Let me, handsome."

Maggie's hand was warm, her fingers delicate. She inserted the tip and ran it up and down her wet slit. Quivering with need, she commenced to slide him up into her. Spreading her thighs wider, she hooked her ankles behind his back. "Ready when you are, my wonderful stallion."

Fargo was ready. He pumped and she thrust, and they climbed to the pinnacle and went over it together, her fingernails deep in the muscles of his arms, her body aquiver with release.

Afterward, they lay a short while, until Maggie sat up and with reluctance remarked, "We can't linger or I'll get in trouble."

Fargo wasn't sleepy anyway. He dressed and adjusted the Colt on his hip and pulled his hat brim lower. He moved to the door and opened it, and couldn't hide his surprise. "What the hell are you doing here?"

Angeline Havard had on a full-length dress and polished shoes, and she was nervously wringing her hands. "I need to talk to you."

"How did you find me?"

McKern stepped around her. "That's my doing, pard. She showed up out front, waving at the window to me. So I went out to see what she wanted, and what she wanted was you."

"So you brought her up here?"

Angeline was staring past Fargo at Maggie, who was insolently arranging her dress and showing a lot of leg and thigh while doing so.

"She said she had to talk to you right away. That it was a matter of life and death."

"Whose?" Fargo asked Angeline.

"Yours."

Fargo turned and smiled at Maggie. "I might see you again on my way back down the canyon."

"I'd like that very much. You give as good a poke as any I've ever got."

"Oh my," Angeline said softly.

Fargo closed the door and took her elbow. "Don't act innocent. I know you're no virgin."

Scarlet crept up her face. "True. But I've never done as she does and sold my body for money."

"No. You sneak around and do it behind your parents' backs, and only with men who share your high opinion of yourself. At least that gal back there doesn't put on airs and give it out like it's gold."

"That was crude," Angeline said resentfully. Then, sighing, she said, "Look. I didn't come here to argue or criticize. I came here because despite what you think of me, I like you, and I'd rather not see you dead."

"That makes two of us."

Fargo led her down the stairs. The saloon was packed. A lot of hungry looks were cast her way. "We can't talk here." He ushered her out, McKern in their wake. A cool evening breeze stirred the dust, and lights were coming on. "All right. Let's hear what you have to say."

"Before I do, I want your word that you won't tell my parents I came to find you."

"Why would I?" Fargo shrugged. "But you have it."

Angeline glanced up and down Yale's busy main street and resumed wringing her hands. "It's about my brother."

"Which one?"

"Allen. He was gone all day, doing God knows what." Angeline bit her lower lip. "I was taking a stroll after supper when someone whispered my name. It was him, hiding in a doorway."

Fargo waited for her to go on.

"I asked Allen what he was up to and he said he was afraid you would do him harm. When I asked why, all he would say was that you were out to get him."

"The weasel," McKern said.

"You looked me up to tell me that?"

"No, no," Angeline said, still wringing her hands. "There's more. You see, I demanded to know what was going on. He said that somehow or other you got it into your head that he was out to harm you."

McKern snorted. "Ain't he slick?"

"Let her finish."

"Allen told me it's because of Strath. That Strath had a grudge against you but you think Allen put him up to trying to kill you."

Again McKern interrupted. "Your brother wouldn't know the truth if it bit him on the ass."

"Allen wouldn't lie to me. I admit he's not a saint. But he's always treated me decently."

"Listen to me, girl. Your brother is a conniving so-and-so. I'd use harsher language but I was raised to treat ladies with respect. Don't you believe a thing he says."

"He's my brother," Angeline said, as if that were enough to justify taking Allen at his word.

"You're taking the long way around the stable to put the horse in the corral," Fargo told her.

"What? Oh. You're suggesting I get to the point. Very well." But Angeline didn't. She wrung her hands and bit her lip and finally said, "Bear with me. This is hard. I don't want to be involved but my brother has left me no choice." She nervously smiled. "I've never done anything like this before."

McKern was growing impatient, too. "Like what?"

Angeline seemed not to hear him. "You see, I care for Allen. I'd never let anyone hurt him. I must do as any sister would do, and protect him any way I can."

Fargo didn't like the sound of that.

"So when he asked for my help, I agreed. He said that he needed to find a way to talk to you, to convince you that your suspicions of him is unjust. But he's worried you'll shoot him on sight."

"I would," McKern said.

"I gave it some thought and came up with an idea."

"Get to the point some time this year," Fargo said.

"Sorry. I'm afraid you won't like it, though. It's the only safe way for him to meet with you." She pointed down the street. "My brother is waiting at the stable."

"Why there?"

"You're to go alone and to give your revolver to me."

"Not likely."

"If you don't, if you show up armed or take McKern along, you'll lose something you value. The only thing I know of that you hold dear."

"What would that be?"

"Haven't you guessed?" Angeline rejoined. "Let me spell it out for you, then. At this very moment my brother is holding a gun to your pinto's head. If you don't do exactly as Allen wants, he'll blow its brains out."

15

Fargo rarely hit women, unless they were trying to stab him or shoot him or kick his face in. He didn't go around slapping women for the hell of it, or to get them to mind, or to punish them, as some men did. It wasn't that he put women on pedestals. He simply didn't treat women any different from the way he treated men, and few women had ever tried to hurt him.

But Fargo came close to hitting Angeline Havard. She was clever, this girl. She had deduced that his Achilles' heel was the Ovaro, and she was right. He had been riding the stallion for years and was as attached to it as any horseman ever got to an exceptional mount. More than that, she had deduced that he would do whatever he had to in order to spare it from harm.

McKern looked ready to slug her, too. "You'd kill a man's horse? What kind of female are you?"

"Not me," Angeline answered. "My brother."

"But you put him up to it," McKern said. "It was your brainstorm."

"All he wants to do is talk. And this way, Skye here won't lift a finger against him."

"You're a damn fool, girl."

Fargo palmed his Colt and held it out. "Hold on to this for me. If he comes out of the stable instead of me, you can keep it. My horse, too."

"Fat chance of that puny pup getting the better of you, hoss."

Angeline put her hands on her hips. "Why are you talking like that? No one is to be harmed. My brother gave his word.

And to prove my intentions, and to show you that my brother can be trusted, I'm going to the stable with you."

McKern shook his head. "It's better if you don't."

"She can come," Fargo disagreed. "And can see for herself how trustworthy her brother is."

Angeline started down the street. She wouldn't look at Fargo although they were practically rubbing elbows.

"What I don't get," he said to provoke her, "is why Allen wants me dead. What's his reason?"

"That's just it. He doesn't. My brother isn't bloodthirsty."

"But he's paid to have people hurt. You said so yourself."

Angeline was angry and struggling not to show it. "Only a few times. And there were special circumstances."

The stable stood by itself, the corral to the rear. Both wide double doors were open and a brilliant shaft of sunlight lit the center aisle. Horses were in every stall and more were tied to posts. Many dozed in the heat. Allen wasn't anywhere to be seen.

"He has to be here somewhere," Angeline said, and called his name. "That's strange," she remarked when there was no answer.

"Better let me go first."

"Not on your life." Angeline moved down the aisle, a hand cupped to her mouth. "Allen? Allen? Where are you?"

A horse whinnied but otherwise the stable was quiet.

"Where could he have gotten to?" Angeline wondered.

The back door was open. Through it, a splash of white and black was visible.

Fargo moved past her. Out of habit, he flashed his hand to his holster—forgetting it was empty. The sun was so bright, he raised his other hand to shield his eyes.

The white and black was indeed the Ovaro. And standing next to the stallion, holding a cocked revolver pointed at its head, was Allen Havard.

"Not another step, scout."

"Go easy on that trigger."

Angeline demanded, "What are you doing? You don't have to point that at his horse."

"It was your idea," Allen said.

"To *threaten* to do it. Not to really shoot the poor animal." Angeline motioned at Fargo. "Look. I brought him, as you wanted. Unarmed, as you insisted. Now talk instead of blustering. It only shows how scared you are."

"Scared?" Allen repeated, and uttered a bark of amusement. "Sis, have you ever known me to be afraid of anything my whole life?"

"I've lost count," Angeline said.

Allen took that as a joke and laughed. "Seriously, now. Why don't you go shopping or something and leave Fargo and me to work this out between us?"

"This was my idea. I'm staying."

"But I don't want you to. It's dangerous. What if he acts up? I'd rather you were somewhere safe."

Fargo had listened to enough. He took a step, saying, "Point that revolver somewhere else."

"Very well." Allen chuckled and trained the Smith & Wesson on him. "I like this better, anyhow. Give me one good reason why I shouldn't squeeze the trigger?"

To Fargo's considerable amazement, Angeline stepped between them.

"Here's your reason. You'll have to shoot me down first. Is that what you want?"

"Damn it, sis. Get out of the way."

"No. I gave him my word you wouldn't try anything, and you will by God stop these childish antics. Here's your chance to convince him you aren't out to kill him."

"I doubt he'll believe me."

Angeline turned to Fargo. "How about it? Will you behave long enough for him to set things right between you?"

"It will take some doing."

"You heard him, sis," Allen said. "Why should I even bother? Please. Go find Father and Mother and leave the scout and me here to settle our differences like men."

"That leaves you out," Fargo said.

"I'm more of a man than my father will ever be," Allen declared. "He's a disgrace to the family name."

"Oh, Allen," Angeline said.

"Well, he is. If you weren't so blind, you'd see it for yourself. Our father, dear sister, hasn't been a man in years."

"Just because he lets mother ride roughshod over him is no reason to talk like that," Angeline scolded.

Allen looked at Fargo. "You know, don't you, scout? Explain it to her. Maybe she'll believe it coming from you."

"What I want to know," Fargo said, getting to the crux of the matter, "is what any of that has to do with me?"

"It has everything to do with you," Allen assured him. "Or don't you remember telling us, before we left San Francisco, that you'll do everything in your power to see to it that all of us make it back alive? Your exact words."

"What's wrong with that?" Angeline wanted to know.

Fargo had a sudden insight. "Your brother doesn't want some of you to make it back. Or is it all of them?" he asked Allen.

"That's ridiculous."

"Then what do you have against me doing what I was hired to do?" Fargo had him. No matter what Allen said, Angeline was bound to be suspicious.

"Yes, Allen. I would like to hear the answer, too."

Allen hesitated. His arm shook from the intensity of his emotion. "God, it would be so easy."

"Allen!"

His face twisted in anger, Allen lowered the revolver with a sharp jerk. "All I wanted to do was talk."

"So talk," Fargo prodded. "Tell me why you paid Strath and Santee to kill me."

"That's just it. I didn't. I can't prove I didn't. But I swear to you I didn't have a hand in either."

"*Somone* put them up to it."

"Why does it have to be me?"

That stopped Fargo in his mental tracks. He'd figured it to be Allen because of how Allen was, and because others had warned him to be on his guard. But what if he was mistaken?

Allen went on. "I admit I'm not fond of you. You treat me like I'm an idiot. But I don't hate you. There's one person who does, though. Hates you enough to do anything to destroy you."

"Who?"

"I can't say."

Fargo was tempted to beat it out of him, but not with Angeline there. "I can make you tell me."

"Skye!" she exclaimed. "Surely you're not suggesting you would beat it out of him?"

"I don't like it when people try to kill me."

"I don't blame you. But you heard my brother. It could be anyone." Angeline smiled. "I want the two of you to shake hands and promise you'll try to get along."

Allen immediately held his hand out. "I'm willing if he is, sis."

Fargo didn't trust him. To show his displeasure, when they shook, he squeezed so that Allen winced and looked fearful Fargo would break his fingers.

"There. Don't you feel better now?" Angeline patted her brother's shoulder and then looped her arm through Fargo's. "Now that that's settled, how about if you treat me to coffee?"

Fargo was thinking. What if she was right? What if Allen wasn't lying? Then who was responsible for the attempts on his life?

"I'm so excited," Angeline prattled on. "In a few days we'll be at Boston Bar. I hope Kenneth is there. I pray we find him alive and well. Maybe he's been writing but the letters don't reach us."

"That could happen," Fargo supposed. Frontier mail wasn't

the most reliable. Hostiles, the weather, coaches that broke down, and horses that came up lame—a host of problems afflicted the express companies. The wonder of it was that *any* mail got through.

The restaurant was small and quiet and relaxing after the hubbub of the street. They sat at a corner table.

"I can't thank you enough for doing that. Don't think I don't realize it took some doing," Angeline said.

"Your brother is lucky to have a sister like you."

"Any sister would do the same. I grant you that Allen can be unbearable. He can be rude and childish and petty. But he's still my brother." Angeline gabbed on about what it was like growing up in the Havard household, and how close she was to Kenneth, and how sad she was when Kenneth and her father had had a falling-out over Cosmo.

"What was that?" Fargo hadn't been paying a lot of attention.

"About Cosmo? Kenneth didn't like the influence Cosmo has over our father. He told Father either Cosmo had to go or he would, and Cosmo didn't, so he did."

"That's when he came north after gold?"

Angeline spooned sugar into her cup. "I don't know if it was the gold so much as Kenneth just wanted to get away. He'd read about the strikes up here and probably decided it was as good a place as any."

"What about you? How do you feel about Cosmo?"

"I don't much care one way or the other. Father has always had manservants. Before Cosmo, there was Bruce. As quiet as a mouse, he was, and so devoted. I don't think I ever saw them apart, not once in ten years. Then Bruce caught pneumonia and died, and father hired Cosmo to take his place."

"Did Kenneth hate Bruce, too?"

"You know, now that you mention it, they never got along very well, either." Angeline sat back. "But enough about me and my family. Let's talk about you. What would you like most in the world?"

"To give you a poke." Fargo didn't know what had made him say it. Maybe it was her lips or how her body filled out her dress.

"My word. Here you go again. But not an hour ago you were poking that saloon girl. And before her you poked that Indian. Don't you ever get tired of all your poking?"

Fargo laughed.

"I must say, you're different from most men I've know. You're much more"—Angeline searched for the right word—"earthy."

"Is that yes or no?"

"You're serious? You honestly think I would let you touch me after I know you've slept with other women?"

"It makes a difference?"

"Maybe not to some women but it does to me. I'm not as promiscuous as they are."

A man entered and looked around. He had dark eyes and a bristly beard and was bundled in a bulky bearskin coat and a beaver hat. He spotted them and lumbered over. Without saying a word he leaned on their table and stared at Angeline. "Here you are. I had to look pretty near everywhere but I've found you."

"I beg your pardon. Do you want something?"

"You."

Fargo sat up. "The lady is with me."

"Do I look like I care?" The man-bear reached a big paw across and gripped a startled Angeline by the wrist. "On your feet. I'm taking you and that's all there is to it."

"How dare you!" Angeline sought to twist free. "Who do you think you are?"

"Folks hereabouts call me Hermit on account of I live off by myself and don't get into town much."

"Let go of her," Fargo warned.

Hermit looked at him. "You annoy me, mister. And those who annoy me, I stomp."

16

Ever since Fargo had arrived in Yale, it had been one aggravation after another. And now this man called Hermit—who smelled worse than a wet dog sprayed by a skunk—marched in out of the blue and grabbed hold of Angeline Havard.

Fargo's temper snapped. He came up out of his chair, his fist arcing, and connected with Hermit's bearded chin. Ordinarily that was enough to drop a man where he stood. Hermit, though, merely staggered, then tossed his head like a mad bull.

"You shouldn't ought to have done that, mister."

"I said to leave the lady be."

"I can't do that. Someone wants to see her, and I'm to take her whether she wants to go or not."

"Who wants to see me?" Angeline asked. "What's this about?"

"You'll find out when we get there, lady. Now come on. On your feet so I can get this done."

Fargo started around the table. "Some people just can't take a hint."

"No, they can't," Hermit said, and reaching under the table, he flipped it over.

Fargo leaped back as the table came down with a crash, narrowly missing his legs. He pushed to get it out of his way.

Already, Hermit had pulled Angeline out of her chair and was tramping toward the door. She dug in her heels and beat on him with her small fist.

"Let go of me!"

Hermit was unfazed. He brushed aside a man in an apron who tried to stop him, and reached for the latch.

By then Fargo caught up. He slammed a punch low on Hermit's back, and Hermit grunted. Fargo drove another blow between Hermit's shoulder blades, thinking it would bring Hermit to his knees.

A backhand caught Fargo across the face, splitting his lip. He felt blood trickling. Wiping his mouth with his sleeve, he waded in again. "You're not taking her anywhere."

Hermit turned. He growled like a riled bear and pushed Angeline to one side. "Stay where you are until I'm done with this pest." He held up both huge fists.

Fargo thought the man was going to box, so he brought up his own. The moment he did, Hermit dived at his legs. Fargo sprang to the right but he wasn't quite quick enough. Iron arms wrapped around his shins and he crashed onto the hardwood floor.

"I've got you now!" Hermit crowed.

Fargo hit him on the cheek and on the shoulders, without effect.

Hermit, undaunted, let go of his legs and lunged, clamping both arms around Fargo's waist. "This will teach you."

Placing his hands on Hermit's arms, Fargo struggled for all he was worth. He might as well be trying to bend rock. Hermit levered onto his knees, pulling Fargo with him, and grinned in Fargo's face.

"Ever hear of a bear hug?"

Excruciating pain spiked through Fargo, from the tips of his toes to the crown of his head. He pushed and thrashed but he couldn't break free. Slowly, inexorably, Hermit's arms clamped tighter and tighter, until Fargo would swear his spine was ready to splinter.

"Finding it hard to breathe yet, pest?"

As a matter of fact, Fargo was. He sucked in a ragged breath. "You can't take her."

"No one can stop me."

It occurred to Fargo that the man wasn't trying to kill, just to keep him from interfering. He slammed a jab to Hermit's chin and thought he broke every bone in his hand. Since all else had failed, Fargo resorted to a nasty tactic; he gouged his thumbs into Hermit's eyes.

Hermit threw his head back and roared in pain. Spinning, he threw Fargo from him with such force that he sprawled onto his hands and knees. He scrabbled to his feet, or attempted to, when suddenly a hand locked onto his chin and another got hold of his hair.

"Ever hear a neck break?"

Fargo thought the pain before was bad; this was worse. He struggled fiercely and couldn't break Hermit's grip. Slowly, agonizingly, his head was being twisted from his neck. He slammed his elbow into Hermit's gut but it was like hitting a washboard. Points of light danced before his eyes and he swore he could feel his flesh ripping.

Then there was a loud crash, and an outcry, and the pressure eased. Fargo sank onto his side. The fireflies stopped swirling, and he saw Hermit with a hand to the back of his head, wearing a bewildered expression.

"Why'd you go and do that for, dang you?" he demanded.

Angeline had hit him with a chair. It lay in broken pieces at his big feet. "You were hurting him!"

"Only because he won't let me do what I came to do," Hermit protested in the manner of a petulant child. "Why are you making it so hard when all I want to do is help?"

"By taking me against my will?"

"Will you come if I ask real nice?"

"I don't want to go with you, period."

"But he told me to fetch you," Hermit persisted. "He said you would be happy to come."

"Who did?"

"I'm not supposed to say."

"But how can I go if I don't know who it is?"

The lines in Hermit's craggy countenance deepened. "All these questions are giving me an ache in my brainpan."

By then Fargo had recovered enough to imitate Angeline. Laying hold of another chair, he raised it aloft.

"Skye, don't!" Angeline darted between them, her arms up to keep the chair from descending.

Hermit turned and glared. "You sneaky cuss. You were fixing to bean me when I wasn't looking."

"Looking or not, it's the same to me," Fargo said, and raised the chair higher.

"No!" Angeline objected.

"I've had enough," Hermit said, talking more to himself than to either of them. "I try to do a friend a favor and I get hit and kicked and beat on with chairs." He stomped to the door and flung it open. "See if I ever do a good deed again." The door slammed behind him.

"What in the world just happened?" Angeline said.

Fargo lowered the chair. "It beats the hell out of me." Inspiration struck, and he grabbed her hand. "Come on."

"Where?"

"We're following your friend to see where he goes." Fargo hurried out and spied the man bear heading up the street; he was so tall he was head and shoulders above most everyone else.

"I've never laid eyes on him before." Angeline began dragging her feet, literally. "Is this wise? He nearly tore your head off. Why push your luck?"

"Wouldn't you like to know who put him up to it?"

That silenced her. Together they threaded through the passersby. Fargo was careful not to get too close. When Hermit suddenly stopped and began to turn, Fargo crouched and pulled Angeline down with him.

"What the hell?" a man said as he nearly tripped over them.

Fargo dared a peek. Hermit had gone on. They followed, Angeline walking so close to him they brushed bodies.

"What if he spots us?"

"Let's make sure he doesn't."

Hermit came to a side street and turned into it. Fargo stopped at the corner and poked his head around. For a few moments he couldn't spot him and he wondered if Hermit had gone into a building. Then Hermit unfurled from next to a hitch rail where he had untied a mule, and after ponderously climbing on, Hermit reined the animal up the street.

"He's leaving town."

"Damn." Fargo let go of her hand. "Get back to the hotel and stay with your family."

"What are you going to do?"

Fargo thought it was obvious. He made for the stable as quickly as he could, saddled the Ovaro, and was back at the side street in less than ten minutes. His hope was that Hermit wasn't in any particular hurry.

Beyond lay a slope dotted with a mix of pines and boulders. A seldom-used trail led up it.

Fargo tapped his spurs. He climbed rapidly and at the top drew rein. The trail led into the mountains, not toward the canyon. He glimpsed a rider just as the man entered timber higher up. From the size, he had to be Hermit.

For the next couple of hours Fargo played cat and mouse. He was the cat, his stalking slow and careful. To the west the sun dipped. When it was poised on the rim of the world, blazing red against a sky of pink and orange, he rode faster to narrow the gap. He didn't want to lose Hermit once dark set in. But he need not have worried.

Hermit didn't go much farther. He turned up a gully that brought them to a strip of timber, and there, hidden among the trees, stood a cabin made of logs and stone. Hermit put the mule in a pole corral. He opened the cabin door and seemed to be saying something to someone inside. Then the door closed.

Fargo slid down and tied the reins to a branch. Shucking

the Henry, he cat-footed nearer. From a window came muffled voices. It sounded like several men besides Hermit were in there. Hunkering behind a trunk, he debated sneaking closer.

The sun was almost gone. The shadows had lengthened. Soon night would fall.

Light flared. A lantern or lamp had been lit. A shadow passed the window and moved back again. It was a man, pacing.

Darkness plunged the timber into gloom.

Fargo was about to drop onto his belly and crawl to the window when the cabin door opened. Out came three men. Not white men, Indians. It looked to him as if one of the warriors did most of the talking and was upset about whatever they were talking about. Finally Hermit and the warrior shook hands, and the three warriors turned to leave.

Fargo flattened. When he didn't hear footsteps, he raised his head. The three had gone past the end of the cabin and were well into the trees. He would lose them if he didn't act fast. He couldn't go after them on horseback; they were bound to hear or spot him. It had to be on foot, and he was loath to leave the Ovaro.

Fargo went to stand and froze. He was so intent on the Indians, he hadn't noticed that Hermit had come out of the cabin and was staring after them. If he stood up, the man would see him.

Hermit gazed up the stars blossoming in the sky. Spreading his big arms, he said out loud, "This would be so much easier, Lord, if people could just get along."

What did that mean? Fargo wondered.

Hermit wasn't done. "But then, I've never had it happen to me, not like he has, so maybe I'd do the same."

Fargo stared after the warriors, who were out of sight. He swore under his breath.

With a loud sigh, Hermit moved to go back in. He paused in the doorway. "I wish them luck," he said, and went in.

Fargo ran to the Ovaro. He would take the chance. He

searched for a quarter of an hour but the Indians were gone. He couldn't track in the dark, so he did the only thing left to him. He rode back to the cabin and drew rein out in front. "Hermit! I know you're in there."

A bulk filled the window and a rifle muzzle was trained on him. "You! How did you find my place?"

"I asked around," Fargo lied. "We need to talk."

"Like hell we do. I should shoot you. I don't like people coming to my cabin unless I say they can."

"What were those three Indians doing here?"

"You saw them? Damn, you're nosy. They're friends of mine. The Knifes and me get along real well."

"What do they have to do with Miss Havard?"

"Who said they did?" Hermit demanded.

Something in his tone told Fargo he had guessed right. "You were bringing her to them, weren't you?"

"Don't be stupid. Anyone who turned a white woman over to the Knifes would be beat to death."

"Then why were you bringing her here? You don't strike me as a badman. You must have a reason."

"I want you to go, mister."

"I can help if you'll let me."

The rifle barrel wagged. "You don't listen very good. I gave my word to keep it a secret." Hermit paused. "But I'll tell you this. It's all the hate that's to blame. It's the hate that kills. And since I'd rather not see any of my friends die, leave it be before you stir that hate up."

"I don't understand."

"I've said all I'm going to." Hermit sighted down the barrel. "I've been reasonable, but if you don't light a shuck, I won't be. Off you go."

Arguing was pointless. Fargo reined around and headed for Yale. The little bit he had learned left him more puzzled than ever. He had the feeling that if he didn't figure it out, blood would flow, and some of that blood might end up being his.

17

There was talk that the British planned to build a road between Yale and Spuzzum by blasting with dynamite. There was also talk of them building a bridge at Spuzzum for the next leg to Boston Bar.

But Fargo and his party didn't have the luxury of a road. They had to follow the narrow, winding, perilous trail that had cost a score of lives since the gold rush. It made for slow going.

It didn't help that nearly everyone was in irritable spirits. Edith wasn't speaking to Theodore and cast barbed looks at Cosmo. Allen visibly stiffened whenever Fargo rode past, as if afraid Fargo would shoot him. Angeline frowned a lot; something was bothering her. McKern kept wanting to use the stock of his Sharps on Allen's head and make Allen confess he had put Santee up to killing them. Rohan was the most cheerful of the entire party, but then he had the packhorses for companions.

Fargo kept trying to make sense of the events in Yale and had to admit to being stumped. The only conclusions he could come to were: Frst, someone was out to kill him and had tried twice, using Strath and Santee; and second, odds were that whoever sent the man called Hermit to bring Angeline to his cabin must be someone who knew her. How the three Knife Indians fit in, Fargo had no idea.

Several hours of beating his head against the problem persuaded Fargo to stop trying. He needed to keep his mind on the treacherous trail. At times it narrowed to where it was barely wide enough for a horse, and it never failed but that the trail was the most dangerous when they were moving along sheer heights, with rapids far below. They had to go slow and, once past the dangerous stretch, wait for the rest to catch up.

Fargo gave orders everyone was to stick together. The young Knifes who haunted the canyon seeking whites to slay could be anywhere.

Allen didn't like the waiting. About the fourth time, when everyone except Rohan had made it across a cliff face and Rohan was picking his way with the pack animals, Allen announced that he was sick and tired of the delays and was going on ahead alone.

"Like hell you are," Fargo informed him.

Allen made a haughty face. "What are you going to do? Shoot me?"

"In an arm or a leg. Then you won't be going anywhere."

Fargo figured the matter was settled and turned to wait for Rohan. One of the packhorses was balking. Eyes wide, nostrils flared, it tried to pull loose of the lead rope. Rohan, superb handler that he was, quietly coaxed the frightened animal toward safety.

"I must admit," Edith said, watching him, "that smelly man is quite good with horses."

Cosmo happened to be hear her and drily remarked, "You can't judge a person by their smell."

"Don't talk to me," Edith said bitterly.

"I wish I could put you at ease, madam."

"I don't want to be at ease when you're around. And you will call me 'Mrs. Havard' and only 'Mrs. Havard.'"

"Honestly," Cosmo said with an exaggerated sigh. "This constant clawing is tedious."

"Go to hell and take my husband with you."

Cosmo went to reply, glanced at Fargo, and frowned. "This isn't the right time or place to talk about that. But I would ask that you keep in mind we are what we are."

"Not in your case, you mouser."

"That applies more to ladies than to gentlemen."

Edith appeared about to hit him. "As if either merits the distinction. How about if I call you a Molly? Or is that too ladylike for you?"

"Please don't be this way."

"There are a lot of other words I can use. But I won't. Despite what you might think of me, I really *am* a lady."

"Why blame me?" Cosmo asked sadly. "Your husband is a grown man and can do as he pleases. Besides, he hasn't asked for a divorce, has he?"

Edith spun around, her fists balled, her face flush with rage. "How dare you? You miserable toad!"

"Let's be civil, madam."

"Civil?" Edith virtually shrieked. She took a step but caught herself and became aware of the stares she was getting. Fargo was nearest, and she looked at him and said sheepishly, "My apologies. It's unseemly to air dirty linen in public. It's just that I've kept it bottled up inside me for so long." She bowed her head and walked off.

"The poor dear," Cosmo said. "She can't for the life of her grasp how it has come to this. She makes the mistake all females do."

"What would that be?" Fargo couldn't resist asking.

"That being female is enough. But there is so much more involved. Theodore is a perfect example."

That reminded Fargo. "Where did he get to?" It was unusual for the pair to be separated.

"He went to look for Allen."

Only then did Fargo realize the younger son wasn't there. Hurrying up the trail, he met the father coming the other way. "Where's your youngest?"

Theodore pointed to the north. "He refused to wait. Frankly, I don't know what got into him. I insisted he do as you advised and stay with the rest but he refused to listen."

"Imagine that." Fargo found McKern and told him to bring

the others on once Rohan and the packhorses were safely past the cliff. Then he climbed on the Ovaro and rode as fast as the winding trail permitted. He was confident he would overtake Allen fairly quickly, but half an hour went by and there was no sign of him. Fargo almost turned back. The fool hadn't listened, so if he ran into trouble, it was his own fault. But Fargo kept riding. Like it or not, he had agreed to get them to Boston Bar. *All* of them, idiots included.

To his right rose tree-covered slopes. Across the chasm was a barren bluff that amplified the roar of the rapids drowning out the clomp of the Ovaro's heavy hooves. Fargo came to a bend. He was looking down at the foam-capped waters and didn't realize what lay beyond the turn until he was almost on top of them.

Allen Havard was on his back in the middle of the trail. His arms were flung out, his open eyes fixed on the blue vault of sky. Blood trickled from a corner of his mouth. More blood, a lot of it, had formed a pool under him. His intestines were oozing from his abdomen.

Allen had been gutted.

The five warriors who had done the gutting were the same young Knifes Fargo ran into before. They were hunkered around Allen and one was cutting at him. The warrior held up what looked to be Allen's heart in his dripping hand.

Fargo drew rein and swung down. Thanks to the roar of the rapids they hadn't heard him.

The warrior holding Allen's heart said something and the others laughed.

Fargo drew his Colt and shot the warrior in the chest. The others spun and came at him, four red wolves out for more white blood. He shot the first in the forehead. The second warrior tripped over the first, and before he could rise, Fargo shot him in the eye. A knife flew past Fargo's neck; he shot the one who threw it. That left the last warrior—the same Knife Fargo had encountered when the prospectors were killed.

"You!" the warrior exclaimed.

"Me," Fargo said, and shot him dead. He replaced the spent cartridges, twirled the Colt into his holster, and stepped over the bodies.

Allen Havard's eyes betrayed the shock of dying. He had been stabbed twice besides the belly wound, and his tongue lolled out. The ground around him was slick with scarlet.

Fargo glanced to the south. It would be a while before the others caught up. He had plenty of time.

Finding a spot to bury the body proved harder than he expected; the ground itself was so hard he couldn't use his hands but had to resort to large rocks and a broken tree branch. A shallow grave sufficed. He covered the body with dirt and rocks and tramped on the mound.

The warriors he dragged off the trail and placed in a row with their arms folded across their chests.

Then came the waiting.

The Havards took the news about as Fargo expected. Edith swooned and, when she was brought around, burst into a flood of tears. Angeline buried her face in her hands and turned away. Theodore knelt next to the grave, his chin on his chest. Cosmo stood behind him and put a hand on his shoulder.

Edith looked up and saw them. The hate on her face was almost inhuman in its intensity.

Fargo roosted on a flat boulder overlooking the rapids and watched the water rush by. He would move on when they were ready.

Boots crunched, and a silver flask was dangled in front of his eyes.

"I reckon you can use a nip, hoss."

"I'm obliged." Fargo took a long swallow and savored the burning and the taste.

McKern wearily sank down. "They came all this way to find a missing son and lost the other one. If life isn't ridiculous it is the next best thing."

"You'll get no argument from me." Fargo treated himself to another swallow and reluctantly handed back the flask. "That looks brand-new."

"I bought it in Yale." McKern drank and gleefully smacked his lips, then caught himself and smothered his glee. "I hope you don't mind."

"Why would I?"

"Don't you remember when we first started out? You laid down the law. You said there was to be no fighting, and to keep the swearing down as there were womenfolk along. Most of all, you said you didn't believe in mixing drink and work." McKern motioned at the men and animals at rest along the trail. "But we're not exactly working at the moment, are we?"

"Don't worry. I won't chuck you in the river."

"In that case, have another chug."

More footsteps approached, and Rohan was there. "Well, look at you two taking your ease."

"I'll let you have a sip but that's all," McKern said. "It has to last me until Spuzzum."

"No, thanks. It's a long way there yet, and I have a lot of skittish critters to nursemaid." Rohan shifted toward Fargo. "It's you I came to talk to. I figured you'd want to know that we have shadows."

McKern squinted up at the sun and then stared at his shadow. "Why wouldn't we? When we're down at the bottom, the canyon might block the sun, but not this high up."

"Not those kinds of shadows." Rohan pointed at the row of bodies. "Those kinds."

"Make it plain," Fargo said.

"We're being followed. Not on the trail but higher up. And not by whites, either."

Fargo resisted an urge to stand and scour the slopes. "You're sure?"

"I wouldn't tell you if I wasn't. At first I'd see a patch of brown and take it for a deer. But it was buckskins."

"Any idea how many?" McKern asked.

"Three."

Fargo immediately thought of the three Indians he had seen at the Hermit's cabin.

"They must be with those you killed," McKern said.

"Maybe not." Fargo didn't elaborate. Either way, though, if the three got word to the rest of the tribe, a war party might be sent to wipe them out.

"I thought you'd want to know," Rohan said. "Now I'd better get back to the horses. I don't want any going over the side."

"Keep a sharp lookout," Fargo directed. "The next time you spot them, send word up to me."

"Will do."

McKern removed his hat and made a show of mopping his sweaty brow, the whole while peering up at the heights. "Want me to sneak up yonder and have a look-see?"

"That's for me to do." Fargo noted the position of the sun. "This delay has cost us. We won't reach Spuzzum by nightfall."

"I'd as soon find a spot to camp. This trail in the dark is an invite to an early grave."

Fargo agreed. Besides, the Havards weren't in any condition to travel. "Stay here. I'm going to scout ahead."

"Shouldn't you take someone? Three Indians is two more than you."

"My Colt and my Henry together hold twenty-one shots," Fargo mentioned. One more if he had a round in the rifle's chamber when he loaded it.

"An arrow or knife with your name on it is all it takes," McKern said by way of a parting warning.

Fargo was glad to be on his own for a spell. The tears were understandable but depressing. He avoided looking up until he had gone about a third of a mile. The only thing that moved was a hawk.

The trail widened and narrowed and widened again before Fargo came to a shelf. The charred remains of previous fires showed it was a popular spot to stop. He kicked at the embers, then climbed back on the Ovaro and rode up the slope to find firewood.

The first stand he came to was an older mix, with plenty of branches scattered about. He climbed down and began gathering a pile. He had almost all he needed when he turned to find a few more.

Without warning three buckskin-clad figures seemed to take form and substance out of the thin air.

One of them knew English extremely well.

"Reach for your pistol and you die."

18

The warrior who had spoken was armed with a rifle and the muzzle was fixed on Fargo. Another had a bow. The third, knives.

Fargo stood stock-still. That they got so close without him spotting them made him want to kick himself. "I won't reach for it if you don't give me cause."

"Says the man who shot five Knife warriors."

Fargo tensed to draw. He figured these three were out for revenge but except for pointing the rifle at him, they hadn't made any threatening moves.

"Don't worry. We saw what they did. They've killed many of our kind. What you did was bound to happen sooner or later."

"'Our kind'?" Fargo repeated. He looked closer and was shocked to his core. The warrior wasn't a warrior at all. Oh, the man was as dark as a Knife Indian and wore the clothes of a Knife Indian but he was *white*. And that wasn't all. Insight washed over Fargo, and he blurted, "I'll be damned."

The man lowered the rifle and came over, his hand offered in greeting. "Yes. I'm Kenneth Havard. Pleased to meet you."

Fargo shook and introduced himself. He glanced at the others, who stood calmly by, and then at the man he had traveled so far to find. He could see some of both Theodore and Edith in Kenneth's eyes and the set of his face. Without thinking he said, "That was your brother those five killed."

"I know."

"You don't seem broken up about it."

Kenneth cradled the rifle. "I'm not. Allen barely tolerated me. He was part of the reason I left San Francisco and came up here. I needed to get away." Kenneth indicated a log. "Why don't we have a seat? I have a few things to say to you, and I imagine you have a few questions."

"More than a few," Fargo admitted.

"My friends will keep watch and see that we're not disturbed." Kenneth addressed the Nlaka'pamux in their own tongue and they moved off as silently as they had appeared.

Fargo eased down, shaking in head in amazement. "I can't get over this. You. Here. And dressed like that."

"The reason is simple, really. But it will take some explaining." Kenneth sat facing him. "Have you ever been in love, Mr. Fargo?"

"Maybe you better start at the beginning."

"Where would that be? With my family? By now you must know how they are. What they are like."

"They don't get along very well."

"That's putting it much too nicely. My mother was always a shrew, but she became worse once father hired Cosmo, and one thing led to another."

"Your mother hates him."

"Does she ever. But she only has herself to blame. If she had been nicer to Father, if she hadn't been such a cold fish, maybe Father would have stayed true to her. Frankly, I'm surprised she never filed for divorce. But then, she's much too fond of money and her creature comforts." Kenneth sighed. "Their situation is another reason I left."

"And your sister?"

"Angeline and I always got along really well. She's a good woman at heart, but if she stays in that household, the hate and the ugliness will taint her."

Fargo gestured at Kenneth's buckskins and hair. "And you?"

"I'm coming to that. I needed to get away but had no idea where to go. The gold rush was in all the newspapers, and practically everyone I knew was coming up here to try to strike it rich. I figured, why not? The adventure appealed to me, and, well—" Kenneth shrugged. "Here I am."

"You came for gold and wound up a Nlaka'pamux?"

Kenneth laughed. "They've adopted me into their tribe. Except for the few who are always out to spill white blood, they are as fine a people as any anywhere."

"A lot of whites don't see them that way."

"And that's part of the problem I faced." Kenneth stopped and gazed down the mountain. "So much hate. Everywhere I go, hate, hate, hate. When I got here I wanted no part of it and kept to myself. I did make a few friends."

A keg of black powder exploded in Fargo's head. "Hermit is one of them?"

"Yes. A fine man, if a bit eccentric. I asked him to bring my sister to me, but she wouldn't come."

"That was partly my fault. He wouldn't say why."

"I asked him not to. I didn't want anyone but Angeline to know I was alive. Father and Mother and Allen would never understand."

"About you going Indian?"

"About me falling in love with a beautiful woman who happens to be a Nlaka'pamux. In our language her name translates as Morning Sun." Kenneth's features softened and a warm glow came into his eyes. "I wish you could meet her. Then you would understand. She is the gentlest of souls. So kind and so caring. There isn't a shred of hate in her entire being."

Fargo sat back. At last it all made sense.

"I was out hunting one day and I ran into her. She was setting snares to catch rabbits. She knew a little English, and we talked. One thing led to another, and before I knew it, I was hopelessly in love." Kenneth paused. "The wonder of it is, she fell in love with me, too."

"You took her for your wife?"

"Not in a church, no. As much as I wanted to, I couldn't. There's too much hate. Any white who acts the least bit friendly toward the Knife Indians is looked down on, spit on, beaten up." Kenneth sighed. "Since she couldn't come and live with me, I went and lived with her. I took up their ways. I married her as they would. I became what you see sitting here before you: a white Nlaka'pamux."

"You've been following us for days, I take it?"

"Since before you reached Yale."

"But how did you find out your family was here looking for you?"

"Teit."

Fargo almost slapped his own forehead. "Damn, I can be dumb."

"She's a good friend. Morning Sun and she grew up together. She brought her grandfather to our lodge and told us about my parents and about you."

More pieces of the puzzle fit together, but there were a few Fargo was missing. "Did you have anything to do with Strath and Santee?"

"Who?"

"Never mind."

Kenneth shifted and placed the rifle across his legs. "I'm taking a chance telling you all this. Teit said she likes you, that you are a man who can be trusted. So I'm trusting you not to tell my father and mother you spoke to me."

"You don't want them to know you're alive?"

"No. Father would try to take me back. He'd do all in his power to ruin my marriage to Morning Sun."

Fargo could see that happening.

"It's my sister I'd like to talk to. If only for a little while. To assure her I'm well and happy and never want to go back." Kenneth looked at him. "That's where you come in. I'm hoping you'll arrange things so I can meet with her in private."

"When and where?"

"I'll leave that up to you."

"Tonight." Fargo figured there was no reason to wait. "I'll bring her up here after everyone is asleep."

Kenneth nodded. "That should be safe. But I warn you. Don't let my father or mother or Cosmo get wind of what you are up to. Especially Cosmo."

"Why him most of all?"

"He's a monster, that one. He's taken over my father and he's tried to take over my father's finances, as well. I've no doubt he would have succeed by now if not for Mother, who has fought him tooth and nail. I sided with her against him and he's resented me for it ever since. I daresay he was delighted when I left home. One less obstacle for him to deal with."

Kenneth stood, and Fargo followed suit.

"Be very careful. I don't want anything to happen to my sister." Kenneth smiled wryly. "I'm doing her a favor and she doesn't even realize it."

"How so?"

"With my brother dead and me pretending to be, my sister stands to inherit a full third of my father's wealth."

"Only a third?"

"There's my mother. And there is Cosmo."

Fargo let that sink in before he said, "You don't care that you won't get any of the inheritance?"

Kenneth shook his head. "All I care about is Morning Sun. I'm happy with her and with her people. They've accepted me as one of their own." He paused. "If there's one thing I've learned living with my father and mother, it's that money doesn't bring happiness. You can have all the money in the world and be miserable."

"I wouldn't mind having a million or so," Fargo joked.

"What would you do with it? For that matter, what would I do with it? Live in a mansion and have servants wait on me hand and foot? Wear only the finest clothes and eat only at the finest restaurants? Where's the joy in that?"

"It would make some folks happy."

"Morning Sun is my happiness. She and I have no need for that much money. We live simply: simple needs, simple passions. I like it that way. I like it more than I've ever liked anything."

Fargo found himself admiring Kenneth Havard a lot. "We're a bit alike, you and I." For him, money had always been a means to an end——to drinking, to poker, to women—not an end in itself.

"I've had to learn my lessons the hard way. And the most important has been that loves comes before everything. Before money and a mansion and fine restaurants." Kenneth shook himself and grinned. "Listen to me. I must sound like a love-struck lunkhead."

"We do what we have to."

Kenneth held out his hand again. "I like you, Mr. Fargo. I thank you, in advance, for any help you can be."

Fargo had a lot to ponder as he tied a bundle of branches for the fire. As he stepped into the stirrups, Kenneth came over.

"I warn you again to be careful. There is more to Cosmo than he lets on. Watch your back around him."

When Fargo came out of the trees he spied McKern leading the others. He reached the shelf before them and had a fire going when they got there.

The sun was low in the sky when Rohan and the pack animals came to a tired stop and Rohan informed them, "I almost lost another one. It slipped and nearly went over the edge."

"Thank goodness you didn't," Theodore said from over by his tent. "I paid good money for those animals."

Several times Fargo caught Cosmo staring at him, but when he looked up, Cosmo always turned away.

After supper, when everyone was sitting around relaxing,

Fargo casually ambled over to where Angeline sat with her neck craned to the heavens.

"Mind some company?"

"Not at all." She gestured at the firmament. "I never tire of the spectacle. I can sit and look at stars for hours."

"How are you at keeping a secret?"

"I've never been accused of betraying a confidence. But why do you ask?"

Fargo made sure no one was near. "I'm about to tell you something. Put your hand over your mouth as if you are covering a yawn."

"That's silly."

"Do it."

"Whatever for?"

"So you don't yell. Or scream. Or make any noise at all." Fargo waited while she complied. "Here goes. Kenneth is alive and wants to talk to you."

Angeline's hand dropped and her lips parted wide and she was on the verge of crying out when Fargo clamped his hand over her mouth.

"Damn it. Didn't you hear me?"

Fargo looked around but no one was paying attention. "Your brother doesn't want your father or mother to know." Confusion replaced her excitement and he felt her relax. "Can I let go now? Have you calmed down?"

Angeline bobbed her chin, and when he moved his hand, she whispered, "Why not tell them? Is he hurt? Is he ill? Is there something else wrong?"

"No, no, and no. He'll tell you himself. For now, act normal and turn in as you usually would. After everyone is asleep, I'll take you to him."

"What about the night guards you always post?"

Fargo had already considered that. "Taken care of."

Things went smoothly.

About an hour after the last person had turned in, Fargo

cast off his blankets and cat-footed to Angeline's tent. All he had to do was scratch the canvas and out she came, a black shawl over her head and shoulders. She went to speak but he put a finger to her lips and shook his head.

He had left the Ovaro saddled. Taking the reins, he walked to the edge of the firelight, then stepped into the stirrups. Reaching down, he swung her up behind him.

"Thank you for doing this," Angeline whispered.

"Quiet."

McKern was by the fire, sipping coffee. He smiled and gave a little wave.

Fargo rode slowly. The less noise, the less chance of anyone hearing. And a single misstep on the slope could prove fatal to the Ovaro. They had gone maybe a hundred yards when Angeline put her lips to his ear.

"I have something to say, so don't tell me to shush."

"It better be important."

"It is. We're being followed."

19

Skye Fargo drew rein and shifted in the saddle. McKern was still sipping coffee by the fire. Sleeping forms covered by blankets were scattered about the clearing. The tents stood undisturbed. "I don't see anyone."

"I'm telling you, someone is following us," Angeline insisted. "I think he dropped to the ground when I turned."

"You think?"

"I'm not ten years old. I saw someone. I swear."

Fargo stayed put, waiting for whoever it was to move. He wondered if it might be a Knife sent by Kenneth to keep an eye on their camp. Or maybe Kenneth himself.

"If it helps, I think it was a white man."

"There you go again."

"What?"

"Thinking."

Fargo received a jab in the ribs for his jest but he didn't take his eyes off the slope. Time crawled by; nothing happened. He reckoned it was safe to go on, and said so. "But keep an eye out behind us, just in case."

"So now you think you believe me?"

"Women," Fargo muttered, and clucked to the Ovaro. He kept glancing over his shoulder but saw no one trailing them. Neither did she.

"I don't understand it," Angeline said at one point.

"The night can play tricks on the eyes," Fargo suggested.

Especially when someone went from firelight into the ink of night, as they had done.

The higher they climbed, the stronger the wind. Funneled by the canyon walls, it whipped out of the north, shaking the pines and occasionally howling like a lonely wolf.

"The wilds scare me," Angeline whispered after a particularly loud howl. "I could never live as you do."

"Your brother can."

"What do you mean?"

Fargo didn't want to spoil the surprise. "You'll find out soon enough. I just hope you're more understanding than Allen would have been." He knew mentioning her dead brother was a mistake the instant he did it. Soon he heard sniffling, and she pressed a cheek against his back. His shirt grew damp from her tears. "When will I learn?"

"I'm sorry. I can't help it. Allen wasn't the best brother who ever lived but he always stood up for me. And he never mistreated me. A friend of mine has a brother who hits her all the time. Allen never did that to me."

"How well did Kenneth and you get along?"

"Fair, I suppose. He's a lot older. Well, six years. So we didn't do a lot together when I was little. I didn't play with him half as much as I did with Allen. But I was sad when he left."

Soon they neared the stand where Fargo had last seen her sibling. He gave the slope below a last scrutiny, then entered the trees. It was so dark he could barely make out his hand at arm's length.

Angeline shuddered. "It's spooky here."

Fargo drew rein. He expected Kenneth and the Knife warriors to pop out of nowhere as they had done earlier, but no one appeared. "Kenneth?" he softly called out.

"This is where I'm to meet him?" Angeline turned from side to side. "Where is he? Why isn't he here?"

"A little patience goes a long way." Fargo had her dismount; then he did. Again he called out Kenneth's name, and again the silence worried him.

"If he said he would be here, he should be here," Angeline said anxiously. "We should look around."

"I'll do the looking." Fargo could just see her stumbling around and tripping and maybe breaking something. "Stay with my horse."

"You're awful bossy."

Palming his Colt, Fargo moved deeper into the stand. He came on a log. As best he could tell, he was at the spot where he had talked to Kenneth but there was still no Kenneth.

An uneasy feeling came over him.

Kenneth had said he would wait there for them. Fargo couldn't see him going off somewhere, not as much as he wanted to talk to his sister. He called Kenneth's name again, quietly, and was mimicked by an anxious Angeline. Walking in a circle, he was soon back at the Ovaro.

"Did you find him?"

"Do you see him at my side?"

"What do we do? Build a fire and wait?"

"A fire can be seen from down below," Fargo pointed out. He hunkered, then reached up, clasped her hand, and pulled. She obligingly sat next to him.

"I don't like this. I don't like it one bit."

Neither did Fargo. The minutes turned into half an hour and half an hour into an hour and no Kenneth.

"I guess he's not coming," Angeline glumly declared. "Maybe we should go back down before my mother or father notice I'm gone."

"They're sound asleep," Fargo said. He couldn't exactly say why but he was loath to leave. "I'm going to have another look around."

"Why can't we look together? I don't like being left by myself. Every rustle is a bear or a mountain lion about to eat me."

Fargo could cover more ground faster alone but he let her help. They had been at it a while when Angeline stumbled. She would have fallen had he not caught her.

"What was that?" she asked.

"You tripped over your own feet."

"No. There's something here." Angeline bent and groped, and gasped. "Oh, Skye! Look!"

Fargo squatted and roved his hand over the ground, or started to. His fingers brushed cold skin and hair, and buckskins. "Hell." He rolled the body over, practically touched noses with the deceased in order to tell who it was.

"Who is it?"

Fargo swore. The cause of death was easy to determine; someone had thrust a knife into Kenneth Havard's throat. Kenneth's own knife was in its sheath. Whoever had murdered him had done it so swiftly, Kenneth had no time to react, no time to pull his own blade and defend himself. Peculiar, Fargo thought.

Angeline flung he arms over her brother's chest, buried her face in his bloody buckskins, and burst into tears.

Fargo let her cry. He searched the rest of the stand for the bodies of the two warriors who had been with Kenneth, but either they had left Kenneth there to meet Angeline alone, or they had gone off in the dark somewhere, and not in the stand. When he came back to the body Angeline had stopped sobbing but was mewling pitiably, adrift in misery. He placed a hand on her shoulder. "I should take you back."

Angeline's long hair swished as she shook her head.

"I'll bury him," Fargo offered to spare her the horror. "In the morning I'll bring you back up if you want and you can pay your last respects."

"I should help." Angeline looked up, her face pasty pale and slick with wet. "God, who could have done such a thing?" She plucked at Kenneth's buckskins. "And why is he dressed like an Indian?"

146

Fargo told her everything he knew. She listened in silent despair, and when he finished, she tenderly placed a hand on her brother's brow.

"To think. He found love, true love, and it was with a savage."

Just when Fargo was starting to like her, she had to go and say something like that. He helped her to her feet.

The burying took a while. The ground was hard. Fargo sweated and grunted and got it done. Angeline helped, stopping several times to cry.

Done at last, Fargo swung up on the Ovaro. He helped her on behind him. She placed her cheek to his shoulder and wept some more.

"First Allen, now Kenneth. This has been the worst day of my life."

Fargo headed down. He was in no hurry. The glow of the campfire was a welcome beacon in a sea of ink.

"We have to find out who did it," Angeline said.

Fargo agreed.

"Which of the Knifes, I mean."

"What makes you think it was one of them?"

"It had to be. Didn't you say two of them were with Kenneth earlier? They're gone now. So it's obvious. One or both of them killed him and the pair took off."

"Nothing is ever as it seems," Fargo said.

"Why are you defending them? You're always sticking up for Indians." Angeline straightened. "It was Indians who killed Allen, wasn't it? So it's perfectly logical they killed poor Kenneth, too."

"Why would they do it?"

"It's simple. He was white and they're red. That's all the excuse they need."

"You're forgetting something. I told you that they adopted your brother into their tribe. They might kills whites but they don't murder their own."

Angeline snorted. "Now you're splitting hairs. Adopted or not, he was still white, and for them, white is evil."

Fargo still couldn't see it, and he told her so.

"Suit yourself. But you have blinders on. You've lived in the wild so long, you think of Indians as people when they're not. They're animals, is what they are. Murdering, butchering animals."

"You're saying that because you're upset."

"No. I'm saying it because it's how I feel. The red race is a blight on God's green earth. We'd all be better off if they were exterminated, as some newspapers have been calling for. Wipe out every last one of them and then there won't be any more scalping and killing and torturing of white people."

"What about the scalping and killing and torturing of Indians?" Fargo countered.

"What's the matter with you? How can you sit there and continue to defend them when we just buried another of my brothers? Honestly. I'm seeing you in a whole new light and I can't say as it's very flattering."

Fargo almost told her to go to hell.

"When we get back to San Francisco, I think I'll write to the newspapers and tell everyone what the Knifes did. And then I'll write to people in government, to important people I've met through my father, and demand they do something about the Indian problem."

"Don't forget to demand they do something about the white problem, too."

"That was petty." Angeline shut up.

Fargo would have kept on arguing to try to get his point across. She needed to understand that both sides bore blame for the mutual bloodletting. That mindless hate was reaping a bitter harvest.

The camp was as they had left it: bundled sleepers, dozing horses, McKern with a tin cup glued to his hand. Smiling, he rose and came to meet them. One look at their faces and his smile faded.

"What's wrong, missy? You look as if your best friend died."

"Close. Another brother." Angeline held out her arms to him. "Help me down, will you? I'm not in the mood to have Mr. Fargo do it."

McKern gave Fargo a questioning look, and Fargo nodded. "Sure, ma'am, whatever you want."

Fargo waited until she was walking off to dismount and ask, "Has anyone been up and about? Anyone left camp that you know of?"

"Not a soul, pard. It's been so quiet I could hardly keep my eyes open. Now what's this about her other brother?"

As they walked toward the fire, Fargo explained, ending, "It has to be one of them." He swept an arm at the sleepers and the tents.

"I don't know. Maybe she's right about the Knifes. Lord knows, they've killed a lot of whites."

"You, too?" Fargo said, and sighed. He poured coffee and drank half the cup in two gulps, then squatted on his boot heels.

"I bet that right about now you regret ever taking this job," McKern commented.

"I told them the risks before we left. They didn't believe it was as dangerous as I claimed."

"That's how most are. They go through life with blinders on, thinking bad things only happen to other folks."

Fargo was raising the cup when McKern gave a start and started to level his Sharps.

"I wouldn't, were I you," said a familiar voice behind Fargo, and there was the click of a gun hammer.

Something hard jabbed Fargo's nape. A rifle muzzle, unless he was mistaken. "What the hell are you up to, Cosmo?"

The manservant came around and stood where he could shoot either of them if they so much as twitched. He was dressed in a shirt and pants but the shirt wasn't tucked in, as if he had thrown them on in a hurry.

"Let's not play the innocent, shall we? I saw you leave, so I followed you. I know what you did."

"What who did?"

"You killed Kenneth Havard. Don't deny it. I saw you huddle with Angeline before I went to bed, and it made me suspicious. So I stayed up and watched out my tent."

"Listen, you've got it all wrong."

"Don't insult my intelligence. I can pull this trigger as easy as anything."

McKern came to Fargo's defense, saying, "How do we know it wasn't you who killed him?"

"What possible motive would I have?"

Fargo answered him. "To get more of the inheritance for yourself."

"You know about Theodore's will? Someone has been talking out of school. I don't like that. I don't like that at all." Cosmo raised the rifle and sighted down the barrel.

20

Fargo threw his coffee in Cosmo's face. As he did, he sprang to one side in case the rifle went off. It did, booming loud in the confines of the canyon, the slug kicking up dirt where Fargo had been squatting.

Fargo's natural inclination was to draw his Colt and shoot the son of a bitch dead. But the rifle was a single-shot. And Fargo wanted answers about Strath, about Santee, and about Kenneth Havard. So instead of shooting him, Fargo swatted the rifle barrel aside and slammed the barrel of his Colt against Cosmo's temple.

Cosmo oozed to the ground, his eyelids fluttering.

The shot roused the sleepers and brought everyone on the run, some rubbing sleep from their eyes, others brandishing weapons. A confused babble arose as they all asked questions at once.

Theodore Havard came shouldering through, imperiously shouting for quiet. Edith was in his wake, tying a robe.

Angeline came running, too, still dressed. She stayed well back, as if afraid her parents would see her and wonder why she had all her clothes on.

Theodore saw the prone form lying in the grass, and stopped in dismay. "Cosmo!" he cried. Dashing forward, he dropped to his knees and put a hand on Cosmo's shoulder. "What is the meaning of this? What happened here?"

"He tried to shoot me," Fargo said.

"What? Why? And you did this to him?" Theodore bent

and shook Cosmo lightly but Cosmo didn't respond. Turning a mask of fury on Fargo, Theodore cried, "If you've killed him, I will see that you pay! So help me God I will!"

Edith had folded her arms and was regarding her husband with undisguised contempt. "Quit making a spectacle of yourself."

"Hush, woman," Theodore snapped. "When I want your advice I'll ask for it." He bent over Cosmo again. "Look. There's a bump on his temple. Damn you, Fargo."

Edith said, "Stop your blubbering. For God's sake, pretend you're a man. Try to act like one for once."

Whipping around, Theodore pointed a bony finger at her. "Bitch. Don't think I don't know how happy this makes you. To see him hurt. To see him lying here. In your eyes he is only getting his just deserts."

"You took the words right out of my mouth, my dear husband."

Theodore appeared about to throw himself at her but instead he turned to Fargo. "I'm waiting for you to explain."

Fargo figured it might as well be now as in the morning. "He thinks I killed your older son."

Theodore recoiled. "Kenneth? You've seen him? Where is he? Are you saying he's dead?"

Surprise was writ large on every face, with one exception.

Fargo noticed and was troubled. He told them about Kenneth. He left out the part about Kenneth not wanting to talk to his parents, and ended his account with his clash with Cosmo.

"Dear God," Theodore said in bewilderment. "Kenneth was alive all this time? And now I won't get to talk to him, to hug him, to tell him how much I love him."

"Oh, please," Edith said. "You never did any of that when he lived at home. But then, you never were good at showing affection."

Theodore stood, his fists bunched. "Speak for yourself.

When did you ever show me any love? From the day we married you were a cold fish. And you only became colder."

"Don't blame this on me." Edith nodded at the figure at his feet. "Put the blame where it belongs."

"How dare you? You were the same before he came as you have been after. If you must look for fault, go look in a mirror."

Cosmo groaned and stirred, and Theodore dropped down and gripped his arm.

"Can you hear me? Are you all right?"

"Fine." Como blinked and winced. "Except for the pounding in my head." He went to sit up.

Theodore bent. "Here. Let me help."

Fargo was watching Edith. Disgust twisted her face, disgust and something else: hate. Hate so potent, her eyes seemed to glow red in the light of the fire.

"God, I loathe the two of you."

"For the last time, woman, shut the hell up."

Edith's lips compressed into a slit. She stared at the sky, and then at the ground, and slid her hands into the pockets of her robe. "Not anymore. I've taken all I can."

"What's that?" Theodore had Cosmo halfway to his feet and wasn't looking at her. "What are you on about now?"

"There is only so much a person can bear. You pushed me into the abyss a long time ago, but I was too timid to do anything about it."

"What are you blathering about? What abyss?"

Cosmo straightened and gingerly touched his temple. "I flatter myself that I understand her, Theodore. Much to my sorrow."

"What else did you expect?" Edith shot back. "God, what a hypocrite you are." Her right hand bulged in her pocket, as if she were making a fist.

"Now, now, my dear," Cosmo said soothingly in that urbane manner of his. "Your problem is that you jump to conclusions. You mistake things that aren't for things that are."

"Save your drivel for my idiot husband. I'm not as gullible. And I'm stronger than you or anyone else ever imagined. I've learned I can do what I have to, and the consequences be hanged."

"I'm afraid you're not making much sense."

"Then let me speak plainly. I hate you. I hate you more than I have ever hated anyone. I hate my husband. I used to care for him but he has killed my love as he has killed our marriage. We're a man and wife in name only. He has shamed me beyond all endurance."

"Typical woman," Theodore said. "Overreacting."

Edith grew red in the face and the bulge in her pocket rose slightly. "You miserable worm. Let me tell you something. When I made up my mind, when I finally decided to do what I should have done years ago, it was a relief. I held everything in for so long, you can't imagine how I felt."

"I have no idea what you're talking about."

"Freedom," Edith said. "To be free of you and the shame. To be free of him"—and she nodded at Cosmo—"and the insult. Fargo was a stumbling block. For all his sinful ways, he's a man of his word. I knew he'd try to stop me. Or take me to the authorities, after."

"After what?" Theodore said impatiently. "What in God's name are you talking about?"

Cosmo had a worried expression. "I think I know but I pray I'm wrong. Reconsider, Edith. What would it get you except years behind bars?"

"Satisfaction. I was going to do it in secret, as I did Kenneth, but now I don't care anymore. Now I just want to be free."

"What was that about Kenneth?" Theodore asked in exasperation. "And free of what?"

"You," Edith said, and her hand came out of her robe pocket holding a nickel-plated five-shot Smith & Wesson .32 caliber revolver. She didn't hesitate. She didn't threaten or posture. She shot her husband in the face. Whether she aimed or by chance, the slug caught Theodore in the left eye and blew his eyeball apart. Before anyone could stop her, she swung toward Cosmo.

"No. Please. I truly cared for him."

"Care for him in hell."

The shot snapped Cosmo's head back. As his legs gave way, blood and fluid leaked from a hole in the middle of his forehead.

Fargo took a step but Edith turned, sweeping her revolver from side to side, covering as many as she could. "I'll shoot. So help me I will." She began to back away.

"Mother!" Angeline pressed through the ring and gaped in horror at her father. "What have you done?"

"What I should have done long ago," Edith replied. She waved her pistol at those in her path and they hastily moved aside. "If I had, maybe your brother would never have left home. He wouldn't have come here and taken up with a red savage."

"You know about that?"

"Who do you think it was stuck that knife in his throat?" Edith rejoined.

Angeline put a hand to her forehead and swayed on her feet. "Dear God, no. Not you?"

"No son of mine was going to take a squaw for his wife. I told him that. I begged him to forget her and come back with us but Kenneth wouldn't have it. He said he loved her. Loved her more than his own family. More than his father and more than me."

Confused, bewildered, Angeline said, "But how—where—when—?"

"When did I talk to Kenneth? After he arranged with Fargo to bring you to him. Apparently he told Fargo he didn't care to talk to your father or me, but he changed his mind. About me, at least. He came down and got me, and I went back up with

155

him. That's when I learned of his squaw." Edith's eyes moistened but she blinked the tears away. "I tried to get him to see reason. I did everything but get down on my knees and beg. But he refused. He intended to spend the rest of his life living with Indians. Can you imagine?"

"So you *killed* him?"

"It was the last straw, coming as it did on top of everything else. Before I knew what I was doing, I had my knife in my hands and I buried it in his neck."

Angeline let out a loud sob. "Oh, Mother. How could you? Your own son? Your firstborn?"

"What do you know?" Edith rasped, and wagged her pistol. "What do any of you know about a mother's love? About a wife's devotion? About the heartbreak when your son and your husband turn their backs on you."

"What now, Mother? You can't kill all of us."

Edith continued to back away. "I haven't thought that far ahead. But I know that now that your father is gone, and that despicable creature who took my place, I stand to inherit a great deal of money. Enough to ensure I never spend a day in jail."

Fargo realized she was moving toward the horse string. So did Angeline.

"Mother, I can't let you go. You must answer for what you've done. I owe that much to Kenneth and to Father."

"Stay where you are. I mean it."

To distract her, Fargo broke in. "Listen to your daughter. You'll never make it back to San Francisco alone. Hell, you won't even make it out of the canyon."

"I might surprise you," Edith said.

Suddenly Angeline ran toward her, crying, "No, Mother! No! It ends here!"

Fargo took two long bounds and was reaching for Angeline's arm when the nickel-plated .32 cracked.

Angeline stopped and bleated, "Oh my!" She covered her stomach with both hands. She looked at him in disbelief and said, "I didn't think she would do it. Oh, Skye." And just like that, she collapsed.

Fargo caught her and gently eased her down. In the few seconds it took, her dress became soaked with crimson. He was conscious of others gathering around, of McKern saying something. Sliding his hand under his pants leg and into his boot, he drew the Arkansas toothpick and went to cut the dress to see how bad the wound was.

"No," Angeline said, weakly gripping his wrist. "Don't bother."

"Maybe I can dig out the slug," Fargo said. "We can stitch you up if we get to it quick enough."

Angeline coughed and blood dribbled over her lower lip and down her chin. "It's already too late. I'm bleeding inside. I can feel it." She switched her grip to his hand. "Oh, God. Hold on to me, please."

Fargo obliged her.

"Skye? Are you there? It's so dark. Why did it have to be like this? I had my whole life ahead of me." Angeline groaned." I don't want to die," she said, and did.

Fargo slowly stood. Those nearest him drew back as if afraid. "Where?" he asked in a voice that wasn't his.

"She took a horse and is making for Yale," Rohan answered.

The saddle creaked under Fargo as he climbed on the Ovaro.

"Wait!" McKern said. "I'll get my horse and go with you."

"No."

Rohan said, "You shouldn't go alone."

Fargo didn't reply. He used his spurs. As much as he wanted to fly in pursuit, it was night and the trail was narrow and he would be damned if he would risk the Ovaro. He rode with caution.

Fargo strained his ears but did not hear her horse. He rounded a sharp bend and the dark ahead thundered twice and lead buzzed his head. Hunching over the saddle horn, he kept going. Her revolver was empty now. There was just Edith and him.

Hooves clattered. She was galloping away.

Fargo continued to use caution. The clatter faded and grew faint with distance. She would have to ride all night to reach Yale by dawn, and he doubted she would make it.

It was an hour later that Fargo came on her exhausted horse standing near the edge of a precipice, the reins dangling. It was caked with dirt as if from a spill.

Wary of a trick, he slicked his Colt out and climbed down. He stood at the brink and from below came a sob. Just one, then silence.

Fargo sat on a boulder. For the rest of the night he didn't move or speak. Not until the sky brightened enough for him to climb down.

She was at the bottom. She had missed the water by a few yards and hit among boulders. Any bones not shattered or fractured were the exceptions. Half her face had been caved in.

He nudged her with his boot and she opened her eyes.

"Fargo? Is that you? Shoot me. Please. The pain. Oh, Lord, the pain."

Fargo turned and started back up.

The screams lasted a good long while.

LOOKING FORWARD!
The following is the opening section of the next novel in the exciting *Trailsman* series from Signet:

THE TRAILSMAN #332
BEARTOOTH INCIDENT

The Beartooth Range, 1861—where no one ever went because the few who had never came back.

It was the worst blizzard Skye Fargo had ever seen, and it was killing him.

Fargo was deep in the rugged Beartooth Range. Mountains so far from anywhere, few white men had ever visited them. He was there on behalf of the army.

"Scout around," Major Wilson had requested. "Let us know what the country is like. Keep on the lookout for Indian sign. And for God's sake, be careful."

It was known that the Blackfeet passed through the range now and then. So, too, did the Crows. Rumor had it another, smaller tribe lived far into the Beartooths, but no one knew anything about them. Like many tribes, they wanted nothing to do with the white man or his ways.

So far Fargo hadn't seen any Indians. He'd been exploring

for six days when the first snow fell. It was just a few light flakes. Since snow in early September seldom amounted to much, he kept on exploring. But the light flakes became heavy flakes, the kind that stuck and stayed if the temperature was right, the kind that piled up fast. Within two hours of the first flake falling, the snow was two feet deep, and rising.

Fargo kept thinking it would stop. He was so sure of it, he went on riding even when a tiny voice in his mind warned him to seek shelter. A big man, he favored buckskins, a white hat, and a red bandanna. In a holster on his right hip nestled a Colt. Under his right pants leg, snug in his boot, was an Arkansas toothpick in an ankle sheath. From the saddle scabbard jutted the stock of a Henry rifle.

A frontiersman, folks would call him. It showed in the bronzed cast of his features, in the hawkish gleam to his lake blue eyes, in the sinewy muscles that rippled under his buckskins. Here was a man as much a part of the wild land he liked to roam as any man could be. Here was a man who had never been tamed, never been broken.

The blizzard worried him, though. Fargo had a bedroll but no extra blankets, and no buffalo robe, as he sometimes used in the winter. He didn't bring a lot of food because he'd intended to fill his supper pot with whatever was handy.

Drawing rein, Fargo glared at the snow-filled sky. A deluge of snow, the flakes so thick there was barely a whisker's space between them, the heaviest snow he ever saw, and that was saying a lot since he had seen a lot. He could see his breath, too, which meant the temperature was dropping, and if it fell far enough, he was in serious trouble.

"Damn," Fargo said out loud.

The Ovaro stamped a hoof. The stallion didn't like the snow, either. Great puffs of breath blew from its nostrils, and it shivered slightly.

Fargo shivered, too. Annoyed at himself, he gigged the Ovaro on. As near as he could tell, he was high on a ridge littered with boulders. Humped white shapes hemmed him in. The game trail he had been following when the storm broke was getting harder to stick to. He hoped it would take him lower, into a valley where he could find a haven from the weather until the worst of was over. Shifting in the saddle, he gazed about. There were no landmarks of any kind.

All there was, was the snow. Visibility was six feet, if that.

Fargo's fingers were growing numb and he took to sticking one hand or the other under an arm to warm it. He tried not to think of his toes. He knew a fellow scout who lost all the toes on one foot once to frostbite, and now the man walked with an odd rolling gait but otherwise claimed he didn't miss his toes much. Fargo would miss his. He was fond of his body parts and intended to keep them in one piece.

Since he couldn't see the sun he had to rely on his inner clock for a sense of time. He reckoned it was about one in the afternoon but it could be later. If the snow was still falling when night fell, he was in desperate trouble. He tried not to think of that, either.

Fargo wasn't a worrier by nature. He didn't fret over what might be. He did what he had to, and if it didn't work out, so be it. Some people were different. They worried over every little thing. They worried over what they should wear, and what they should eat, and what they should say to people they met, and they worried over how much money they made, and whether they were gaining too much weight or going gray or a thousand and one other anxieties. They amused him no end. All the worry in the world never stopped a bad thing from happening. But Fargo had cause to worry now. He would die if he didn't find somewhere to lie low until the worst was over. He would succumb to the cold and his flesh would rot from his bones and one day, perhaps, a wandering Indian or white man would come on his skull and a few other bones and wonder who he had been and what he had been doing in the middle of nowhere and why he had died.

"Enough of that," Fargo scolded.

It helped to hear his own voice. To remind himself he was alive, and a man, able to solve any problem Nature threw at him. He had never been short of confidence.

So on Fargo rode, looking, always looking, for a spot to stop. An overhang would do. A stand of trees, even. A cave would be ideal but it had been his experience life was sparing with its miracles.

More time passed. The only sound was the swish of the falling snow and the dull clomp of the Ovaro's heavy hooves.

The cold ate into Fargo. By now the snow was three feet deep in most places, with higher drifts. The drifts he avoided, if he could. They taxed the Ovaro too much, and he must spare the stallion.

Huge white shapes appeared. Boulder as big as log cabins.

Fargo had no choice but to ride between them. As he came out the other side, he nearly collided with a rider coming the other way. Instantly, he drew rein. So did the other man.

Squinting against the lash of snow, Fargo could make out the dark outline of the man and the horse, but nothing else. His hand on his Colt, he kneed the Ovaro alongside.

It was an Indian.

An old warrior, his hair nearly as white as the snow, his craggy face a testament to a life lived long and lived hard, studied Fargo as Fargo was studying him. He, too, wore buckskins, only his had beads on them. His mount was a pinto. It had black-and-white markings, like the Ovaro, only the patterns were different.

Fargo stared at the old warrior and the old warrior stared at him, and neither said anything. Fargo didn't see a weapon but no one, red or white, went anywhere unarmed.

The old man trembled. Not from fear, for there wasn't a trace of it on his face, but from the bitter cold.

Fargo looked closer and realized the old man was gaunt from hunger and haggard from near exhaustion. The eyes, though, were filled with a sort of peaceful vitality. They were wise eyes. Kind eyes.

"Do you speak the white tongue?"

The old warrior simply sat there, a shivering statue.

"I reckon not," Fargo said. Twisting, he fumbled with his cold fingers at a saddlebag and got it open. Rummaging inside, he found a small bundle of rabbit fur. Carefully opening it, he counted the pieces. He had six left. That was all. Without hesitation he took three out. He wrapped the rest and put the fur back in his saddlebag, then held out his hand to the old warrior.

"For you."

The old man didn't move.

"It's pemmican." Fargo motioned as if putting a piece in his mouth, and then exaggerated chewing. He held the pieces out again. "They're yours if you want them."

Caked with snow, flakes clinging to his hair and his seamed face, the old warrior stared at the pemmican and then at Fargo and then at the pemmican again. Slowly, as if wary of a trick, he extended his hand.

Fargo placed the pieces in the old man's palm. He asked in Crow who the old warrior was and then in the Blackfoot tongue and then the Sioux language, which he knew perhaps best of all Indian tongues from the time he lived with the Sioux. He tried a smattering of other Indian languages he knew.

The old warrior just sat there.

Fargo resorted to sign language. Fingers flowing, he made the sign for "friend" and asked the man's name.

The old warrior never moved nor spoke.

"I don't blame you for not trusting me," Fargo told him. Not given how most whites treated Indians. "I'll be on my way, then." He didn't want to. The warrior might know where to find shelter from the storm.

Touching his hat brim, Fargo rode on. He didn't anticipate an arrow in the back, but he glanced over his shoulder to be safe and saw the old warrior staring after him. Then the snow closed in.

Fargo sighed. He had half a mind to turn around and follow him. The old man must know the mountains well. But it was plain the warrior didn't want anything to do with him.

Suddenly the Ovaro slipped. It recovered almost instantly, and stopped.

Fargo leaned to one side and then the other, bending low to examine the ground. He couldn't be sure because of the snow but they appeared to be starting down a slope. The footing was bound to be treacherous and would become even more so if ice formed.

"Some days it doesn't pay to wake up," Fargo grumbled. He gigged the Ovaro.

The next hour was the worst. The snow never let up. Twice the Ovaro slipped, and each time Fargo feared he would hear the snap of a leg bone and a terrified squeal.

He was terribly cold. His skin was ice and when he breathed, he would swear icicles formed in his lungs. His feet were numb, his hands slightly less so. He shivered a lot. His body temperature was dropping, and once it reached a certain point, he was as good as dead. There was a word for it, a word he couldn't recollect. But the word didn't matter. A person died no matter what the word was.

Fargo never thought he would end it like this. He'd always imagined going down with a bullet to his brain or his heart, or maybe an arrow or a lance. But not in the cold and the snow. Not by freezing to death.

The Ovaro slipped again, and this time it wasn't able to regain its balance. Fargo felt it buckle and he instinctively threw himself clear of the saddle. Or tried to. For in pushing off, he slipped on the snow-slick cantle and pitched headlong to the ground. He figured the snow would cushion his fall but he didn't land in snow; he came down hard on a snow-hidden boulder, his shoulder bearing the brunt, and pain shot clear through him.

The next moment he was tumbling and sliding.

Fargo envisioned sliding over a precipice and plummeting to his doom. He clawed at the ground but all he could grab were handfuls of snow.

A white mound loomed, another boulder, and he careened off it and hurtled lower.

Dazed and hurting, Fargo sought to focus. He thrust his hands into the snow but it had no effect. In fact, he was gaining speed, going faster every second. Fargo swore. Sometimes a man did all he could and it wasn't enough. Some folks gave up at that point. They figured, What was the use? But Fargo never gave up. So long as he had breath in body, he fought to go on breathing.

Rolling onto his stomach, he jammed both arms and both legs into the snow.

It didn't work. The snow was too deep. No matter how hard he tried, he couldn't reach the ground. He couldn't find purchase. All there was was snow and more snow.

Fargo had lost sight of the Ovaro. It could be lying above him with a broken leg. Or maybe it was sliding down the mountain, too. He vowed to go look for it. Provided he survived.

Another mound loomed. Fargo threw himself to one side but the snow had other ideas. His other shoulder slammed hard. The pain was worse than the first time. Now both of his arms were numb. He had to struggle to move them even a little.

And he was still sliding.

His hat was gone, too. That made him mad. A hat was as necessary as footwear. It shielded a man from the heat of the sun and the wind-whipped dust and falling rain. He'd had that hat for a couple of years now and managed to keep it in fairly good shape.

Fargo peered ahead, seeking some sign he was near the bottom. He had the illusion he'd slid half a mile but it couldn't have been more than a few hundred feet.

Suddenly he shot off into space. He looked down but saw only snow. Flakes got into his eyes, and his vision blurred. He tried to twist so he wouldn't land on his head and neck but he was only partway around when he smashed down with a bone-jarring impact. If he counted on the snow to cushion him, he was wrong. It felt like his chest caved in. He slid he knew not how many more feet and crashed against a boulder.

God, the pain! Fargo hurt all over. He thought half his bones must be broken. He marveled he was still conscious, and attempted to sit up. The attempt blacked him out. For how long, he couldn't say, but when the stinging lash of falling snow revived him, the sky was darker.

Night was falling.

Fargo had to get up. He had to keep moving. If he stayed there he would freeze. His days of wanderlust, of roaming the frontier wherever his whims took him, would be done. He got his hands under and pushed but his strength had deserted him. He rose only as high as his elbows and then fell back.

"Not like this, damn it."

Again Fargo sought to rise. Again his body betrayed him. He lay, staring up into an ocean of falling flakes, his consciousness swirling like the eddies in a whirlpool. He felt himself being sucked into a black abyss and there was nothing he could do to stop it.

Nothing at all.

No other series packs this much heat!

THE TRAILSMAN

**Follow the trail of the gun-slinging heroes of
Penguin's Action Westerns at
penguin.com/actionwesterns**